I0633320

THE 13TH FLOOR

A HALLOWEEN STORY

JACK STEEN

DEATHBED PUBLISHING

CONTENTS

INTRODUCTION

This asylum has always had a missing floor.

The thirteenth.

Every Halloween, the building unlocks the door, and this time, it was my turn for an invite.

I would have turned down the invite, but I wasn't given a choice.

And when the doors opened, I met a man waiting in the dark.

Pastor Cole. A killer who preached salvation and killed you with a smile.

I've heard a lot of confessions from the dying, but his was different. He didn't want forgiveness. He wanted witnesses.

He said the thirteenth floor was his church--that the voices behind the walls were his congregation.

He said the Matron still keeps his sermons running.

Now the lights hum, the walls breathe, and something keeps whispering my name.

I should've never stepped into that elevator.

The 13th Floor -- every floor has a secret. Only the 13th keeps the dead.

THANK YOU

Special thank you's to the following **Long Term Patients, Ward Members and Asylum Addicts** from my VIP ADDICTS. This book would not be possible without your support!

New Patients:
Chloe Lynn, Paulina, Katie, Linda Tervo, Laura Tilley, Holly, Veronica Garcia, Helena Hunter, Jennifer, Cheryl, Marianna Beverdige, Irene Roberts, Savannah Hong,
Lisa Fedel, Alfie Lodge

Long Term Patients:
Tina, Keebler Hammons, Taunya Hazen, Mama Bear, Elizabeth Trowbridge, Treven Rittenhouse, Sarah, Kimberly Kramer, Chelsea May, Jodi, Cathulhu13, Kristen Prevondoski, Laura Hays, Lola Stracke,
Kimberly Holland, Dominique Aragon, Helena Hunter, Julie S, Samm, Beth Ford, Raychelle Davis, Jeannie Greer, Kimn, Lisa Dawn, April Huff, Skye Seeland

Ward Members:
Tara Lansing, Amanda Hicks, Heather New, Jessica Hawkins,

Josie, Amy Harwick, Ashlee, Wendy Elgie, Luna, Gaby Lyons,
Leslie Weimmer, Feyra Stalica,
Allie Johnson, Constance Gray, Kendra M, Omega Urban,
Fai Rose, Candice G, Terry Schott, Cheryl Graham, Brandi75,
Eyvette, Liv Paolacci, Linsay O'Hare,
Lisa Anderson, Autumn Burns, Kaitlin Morris,
Tracy Gibson

Aslyum Addicts:
Ambone, Abi Willshee, Chiffon Cameron, Crystal Gillette, SG,
Bianca Van Slingerland, Kim Coughlin, Sage Steel, Kaylee Brown,
Andrea, Kelly Folz, Tricia, Misty Moon, Brittney Gurley,
Brookuskatookus, Tammy Woods,
Miss Maxine, Alicia S, Cheryl, Misty, Kristen Simpson,
Kristena Peters, Maryanne, Megg, William Adkins, Rachel Miles-
Davis, Eric Pokrovsky, Jessie Alfano, Darian, Terea Rascoe,
Valentinova Luttner, Krystal Walker, Kerra Waldenmyer, Dana
Cross, Jennifer, Natasha Gray, Kristena Hodge, Tanya Jack,
DeAnna Ash, Brandy Plecki, Amy Keifer, Jordan Hooten, Jen
Brooks, Ashley Lewry, Kymberly Berg, Taylor Gunter, Asya
Hudson, Crystal Beck, Ayira Moon, Maegan Rathbone, Dara
Duncan,
Arial Beaulac, Kimberly Oates, Natasha Smith, Lynn Collins,
Narcoloc, Phillip McAtee, Mistie Walker, Samantha Bess,

These confessions are dedicated to you!

JOIN ME

I'm just going to throw this out there: there will be more books. But while you wait, why not join me over on my VIP ADDICTS group?

What happens over there? A lot. Like…you read these confessions before anyone else. Like…you get to name characters. Like…you get free books.

It's also a better way to stay in touch rather than a mailing list that you may or may not see in your inbox.

https://www.patreon.com/jacksteen

Click to check it out…no pressure, but if you do sign up, be sure to say hello in one of the posts, and I'll raise a toast to you at the pub.

WHO AM I?

Hey, thanks for picking this one up.

I bet we have something in common - we both have a thing for the darker stories.

I bet Halloween's your favorite time of year, too. Mine definitely is. Something about the chill in the air makes people honest. The masks may go on, but we see what's beneath, and personally, I find that more interesting than anything else.

I'm **Jack Steen**—night nurse, record keeper, professional listener. The patients on my floor call me the Death Angel. It's not a compliment. I deal in death. Specifically, deathbed confessions - if you don't know that by now, check out my Asylum Confession books and read the deathbed confessions of monsters. I'm sure you can handle them.

My ward? Let's just say it's the floor where the dying end up—the ones the world forgot, the monsters everyone pretends never existed. They come to me when they're ready to confess. And I listen. That's all I do.

I won't tell you where the hospital is. Doesn't matter. They're all the same. You'll figure it out if you're paying attention, but saying the name out loud? That's the kind of thing that gets people sued—or worse.

You want to know why I do this, why I sit with killers while they choke out their last words. Truth is, I don't know anymore. Once, I thought I could save people. Now I just keep them company until the silence wins.

Here's how it works: They live downstairs, locked behind doors and diagnoses. But when the end comes, they're wheeled up to me. I give them their meds, change their sheets, and let them spill their guts one last time. They call it care. I call it bearing witness.

I won't tell you their real names, only the ones I give them— the ones they earn. Some stories are lies. Some are truths wearing masks. But if you're smart, you'll read between the lines.

Because the walls remember, and on Halloween night, the walls always talk the loudest.

WHAT YOU'RE ABOUT TO READ...

This book you've picked up is a little... different.

There's a confession, for sure.

There's Halloween - which we all love.

But there are some other things that have been included that might not make sense at first, but once you finish this book, it'll all become clear.

Just trust me.

To begin, I've got a short story for you—well, not really a story, but more of a record—which I explain below. Then you'll read about Ephraim Cole and the 13th Floor. Another short story/record will complete everything, and some found transcripts/ledgers are mixed in.

It'll make sense as you read through.

They tell me every hospital keeps two ledgers: one for the living, one for the ones who don't stay that way. Most people never see the second. I did.

This story—*The Matron's Census*—isn't one of my usual confessions. It's a record. A leftover. I found it wedged behind the drawer in Records B, typed, unsigned, but easy to recognize. The handwriting on the margin matched a name we all know, even if no one says it after dark: **Matron Hale.**

The Board called her "efficient." The staff called her "unlucky." The patients? They just called her *Ma'am*—and prayed she wouldn't count them twice.

Every Halloween, the vents hum a little louder on the night floor, and the bells ring when no one's touching them. The rest of the staff blame the pipes. I know better. The building still does its census.

So, if you're reading this, remember—this isn't a ghost story. It's payroll. And the Matron's still on duty.

THE FIRST RITUAL

THE MATRON'S CENSUS

(A Ward C Journal by Matron Margaret Hale)

I. Preparation

19:00. The bell sits on my desk like a tame animal, brass cooled by October. I polish it until I can see my mouth in the curve. It warps my lips into a stranger's shape. Good. The building believes strangers. The building listens when you are not precisely yourself.

Supper trays gone, bed checks completed, sedatives administered to those who insist they do not need them. Mr. Talley kept his hidden under his tongue until I pressed the spoon and watched the pill surrender to paste. He glared at me as if hate were a secret he could keep. You cannot keep secrets in an institution. That is the point of an institution.

On the blotter, tonight's census card lies ready: twenty-eight names, two blank lines for emergent admissions who will not arrive and never do on All Hallows; the ward knows better. Above the card, I have placed the ledger—the Nightingale ledger, my invention by the Board's decree, which mostly means they have discovered a way to measure me. "Every number is a life, every life a record." They have begun to quote me back to myself in committee. I do not correct them. It is policy's job to forget who first said a true thing.

There are bats in the nurses' lounge upstairs—paper ones, dangling by thread from the tin ceiling grid. The girls wanted to cut pumpkins for the windows. I told them no. Children's faces are a bad practice here. A pumpkin is only a child's face once removed.

The floor plan I did not request arrived by pneumatic tube at ten past six. It shows a corridor I do not recognize between twelve and fourteen. A thin band of hallway with no rooms, labeled simply M-13. Not a floor, then. A notch. A breath between. Someone has signed the bottom: *Carrow, Eng.* I do not know a Carrow.

The tube coughed after, as if it had choked on paper. I held the plan to the light and saw the ink filmed with the faintest ash. The elevator has never admitted a thirteen, the buttons skip the way superstitions do. The plan admits it. The plan has less pride than the lift.

I ring my bell once, and the sound goes up through the vent and does not come back. That is good. If it returns, it has learned your name; if it does not, it is still choosing one.

I write at the top of the ledger page: **All Hallows' Eve. 1956. 19:12. Begin.**

The radiators sigh in chorus. It smells like bleach and boiled wool. Somewhere in the north wing, a radio plays "Autumn Leaves" three tones off—maintenance tunes nothing and everything. The building swallows tunes and hums them back into itself.

Tonight, I will give the hospital the names, and the hospital will keep or release whom it wants. I am not a priest. I am a counter. I am the woman who marks the tallies when an unruly God decides to keep score.

I take up the bell. It nests well in my palm. I think of it as a heart removed for weighing. I teach my girls to ring it with the wrist, not the arm. Less theater. More truth.

"Every number is a life," I say aloud, so the line will hear who first spoke it.

The vent above my desk exhaled once, as if amused.

I begin.

II. The Counting Begins

19:30. The light in Ward C is the color of paper. We keep it thin to make the dark patient and the day humble.

Bed 1: Mrs. Carden. Teeth like stones under the lip, hands making anxious nests in the coverlet. "Mrs. Carden," I say. "Eleanor. Present." I ring, a palm's turn, and watch for the echo. The vent near the ceiling mouths her name back without sound. I tick the ledger. A cross mark. Present.

There is a rhythm to the census. You measure the ward's pulse and decide if you are setting it or if it is setting you.

Bed 2: Mr. Lait. He tells me every Sunday that Jesus will come on a Tuesday. "This is Wednesday," I say, and he nods, relieved, spared another disappointment. The bell answers him with three beats and a pause, so faint I could pretend it is my own blood. I do not pretend. I make the second mark.

Bed 3: open. Bed 4: the widow who is not, but insists on the respect. "Widow Hayes," I say, because sometimes your name is not in the chart but in the mouth that calls you. She smiles without teeth and lets me count her breath. Eight, steady.

I move—names spoken softly, like I am coaxing them out from under their beds. Names whispered like stitches. The bell makes a seam along this aisle, then the next.

A moth has found our light and spends itself along the long bulb above the nursing station. It taps in a quick code: three, then one—census rhythm. I make a note in the ledger. Things learn our patterns. Things teach them back.

The girls tread like careful cats past doors that do not close well. We do not latch anyone in on this night. The locks stick, the hinges complain, and I will not have the ward decide it is the jailer.

At Bed 12, Mr. Boone stares at the vent in the corner as if it has spoken. "Save me a place," he says not to me. "There aren't enough chairs in the chapel." I do not correct him. I mark his name and the bell stutters once, a spoon on the rim of a glass.

There are names that do not wish to be called. We carry them gently. We do not lift the wrong corners of their sheets. We let them count us, too—our steps, our rings, our little patience, and our big.

At the end of the second aisle, the world of Ward C closes like a lid. You feel it always on this night—the sense that the windows look onto hallways instead of sky. We hung a paper moon last year to trick the patients into night's shape. The building tricked us back by doubling it in the medicine cabinet mirror. Two moons that night, one with a slit for a mouth.

At the end of the third aisle, the vent opens its throat long enough to learn me again. The voice in there is my own cadence played back: three, pause, one. The bell on my desk upstairs answers once, faintly, as if I were in two rooms, as if tonight I have help.

I write in the ledger: *Assistance registered: ARP—census pattern.*

I do not write that the pattern steadies my hands. There is a superstition that the Matron does not shake. I do not shake. It is only the bell, shivering like a creature that wants to be used.

When I turn the last corner of the ward, there is a door that is not. It is where the linen closet has always been. The closet knows its place. Tonight it has become a threshold—frame and sill and a number above it: 13-C. The paint looks wet. The brush that wrote the 13 stuttered as if caught by a breath.

I ring my bell once, the gentle way, the way we wake those who do not wake. I say no name because none belongs there.

The vent above the new door whispers a simple, polite thing: *Matron.* The sound does not come down. It goes up.

I open the door.

III. The Unlisted Patient

20:15. The room beyond the unnumbered number is not ours. The height is wrong. The walls are closer, and the tile is grooved by feet that weighed more than our lives do now. Medicine leaves marks. Medicine is a handprint right where you cannot wash.

A bed is centered, arranged as if for a photograph—taut and steady. On the sheet, a mound the size of a person. The mound breathes in sync with my count. In, two, three; hold; out. A disciplined breath, the kind that sits still for a ruler. I ring the bell, and the mound stops breathing for one beat, then resumes as if we've agreed on a tempo. Maybe we have.

"Name," I say. It is not a question. A census is not a conversation. It is a wall of small doors, and you open each to see what number sleeps there.

The vent over this bed is the older kind—shallow slats, paint gobbed on by rollers instead of the careful brush. It has teeth. It simply shows them, white with dust.

"Name," I say again.

The mouth in the wall says, "*Yours.*"

I do not drop the bell. I have not dropped the bell in sixteen years. I put it down deliberately, as one puts down a hot pan. I open the ledger and the pencil thinks without help: **Margaret Hale, Matron C. Present.** The pencil writes like a little bell.

"You are not in your bed," I say to the mound, and smooth a wrinkle near the feet to prove I am practical. The cotton is cold. There is nothing in the sheet. I know this because my hand meets its own emptiness, and still the bed breathes.

The building shifts its attention. The feeling is no less than stepping into a chapel when the congregation has already begun to sing. Your name is not called, but the harmonies have made a gap in the sound where you must stand. It would be rude not to.

I go to the wall and rest my ear to the vent. It hums. It hums my bell tone and then something older, a seeing-glass of a sound, the frequency the organ tuner chases and never catches.

The old intercom clicks on. It has not worked in a month. The girls told me; they wanted a new one, portable, battery-fed, for rounds. I told them no. The box on the wall jerks itself into function, and a woman's voice—mine, but older, or the person I am when I am tired—says into the room: *All accounts will reconcile in blood.*

It is not prayer. It is not doctrine. It is bookkeeping. The work of a night nurse. The work no one wishes to read about in the newsletter.

I count the breaths under the sheet aloud so the room knows I am still the one with the pen. Eight. Nine. Ten. The tenth beat bends a little, like a picture in rippled glass.

"Show me the patient," I say.

The vent offers me the smallest gift it can—a draft, the smell of iron and milk. A lantern's idea of light pools on the floor, a stain with no source. In the reflection of that brightness, the bed holds a woman my shape, her hair pinned wrong—two bobby pins crossed like blades. She does not look at me directly. The eyes are for someone above, for a balcony of listeners, for the ceiling.

"Name," I say the third time, and I ring the bell in the wrong way now, the way that calls a doctor who will not come.

The woman in the bed mouths *Margaret* and the vent says *present.* The ceiling answers with a shallow bell, the kind used on a desk when no one wishes to shout.

The ledger writes itself for one line. The pencil simply moves. It is unremarkable. It is what hands do in institutions when you have made a rule so often that the body performs it without supervision. The words say: **13-C. Intake. Stewardship confirmed.**

I put my hand flat on the page to stop it. The paper is warm. Warm like the underside of a wrist. The building has begun to take care of itself and has asked only that I supervise. I can supervise anything. That is the pride and the sin of a Matron.

Behind the glass, the woman settles deeper into the cot that does and does not exist. Her breath and mine slide into unison. Dancing lessons, years ago, my mother's hand on my waist, my palm on her shoulder, the feeling that I could make the room move if I stood up well enough.

"All right," I tell the room. "If I am the name that opens this door, then let us finish properly."

I ring the bell once, soft. The vent learns an octave lower.

I make a mark in the ledger: *Unlisted patient: accounted.*

Outside the door that is not a door, the ward rustles. Boots. The light shifts. Someone tries the handle. It does not have a handle. It has never had a handle. The ward corrects someone, and they drift away, embarrassed by a mistake they cannot name.

There is work to do. There is always work to do. I leave the room that is not in our inventory and take the night, like a sheet, between my hands, tucking it in at the corners.

IV. Confession and Combustion

23:55. The ward changes temperature the way a fever does—incrementally and then all at once. The metal of the bell stings my palm with cold and then warms like a breath held too long. A moth singes itself on the light and leaves a brown comma. I measure the pause between the bell tones through the vent and realize it matches my heart when I lie. I am not lying. The vent is lonely and has invented an error for company.

The last aisle's last bed belongs to nobody. We keep it made, perfect. We pretend the linen is not waiting for a name to print itself. On this bed, every All Hallows, we place the ledger for the counts to ride through to the morning. The book loves this bed, the way some books love tables made from their cousins. I lay the book down. The pages flutter like a chicken run without its head; ugly; precise.

"Eight," the intercom says in my voice. "Of eight." It is a prayer in arithmetic. It is a sentence without a noun. Completion is its own subject.

The radiators stop their gossip mid-word.

The light in the vents brightens as if someone has pushed a lamp, a foot, a child, through the duct. The air turns to breath. My girls step out from the nursing station with their mouths shaped for calling my name and cannot say it because the air in their throats has been marshaled into marching. You cannot speak when you are recruited by a drum.

"Girls," I say. "To stations." This is the order I have used during a lightning strike, an escape attempt, a death. The order that makes everyone remember we are the adult in the room.

I smell smoke. Not the big smoke that speaks in shout. The thin smoke of dress silk touched by a candle. The building tries on fire like a shawl, drapes it over one shoulder, and asks us what we think.

We think no, thank you.

But the duct knows a way out of every wardrobe.

Past the nurses' station, the linen chute hums like a girl at her work. It is an old chute, an iron door, and difficult. I have never liked the paint on it. It scabs. Tonight, it shows a fever of color: orange at its edges, then a skein of red as if a child had taken a crayon to the seams. It puffs a little every time the vent says *present*.

"Matron?" says Ruthie, who sings psalms in laundry and lies about liking boys. She is very brave and has never learned to be quiet. "Matron, what is it?" She has a mop, ridiculous as that is—mops do not fight fires; they conduct them.

"Names," I say. "Finish the names." I do not raise my voice. The ward obeys the quietest person.

We speak. The girls offer the last few names like coins at a toll. The vent counts with us, penny, penny, penny, a pause for the Lord's cut. When the last name is spoken, something behind the linen door remembers it has a mouth.

The chute exhaled heat with intention. The bell—my bell—rang by itself. A thin note, almost embarrassed, and then—oh then—the wall learned to sing. Not song-like tunes. Song like someone who has found the same note in their throat and in their home.

Fire is not the right word. Combustion is better. Light without flame. A joy of heat. The ward does not burn. The ward remembers burning and does it again in outline, the way a child retells a story, only with the best parts. I walk to the linen chute and place my palm on the iron. I can feel something moving behind it. Children, my girls, the old, the ones with paper hearts—they all whisper in the ducts with the exact same timbre. A hospital teaches timbre. You leave here speaking one note lower and one note older.

Somewhere a switch trips. The intercom makes a formal cough. "All accounts," says my voice, "reconcile in blood."

"I have balanced eight," I tell the wall, because one must speak back to an intercom or risk forgiveness. "I have measured breath and counted the confused and the angry and the dutiful dead. I have kept your book. Let go."

The vent answers in a sound like a thrown spoon. Three beats. One. Then a chime not our own—the chapel's desk bell, rung from a hand without a desk.

Paper lifts in a wind that comes from nowhere. The ledger's page licks my knuckle. The pencil slides like a small fish. I put my other hand on the book and hold it like a pulse.

The bed under the ledger changes shape. The mattress bows as if someone heavier than I am has sat to rest. The light in the duct goes calm. Not out. Calm, the way a chest goes when confession ends.

"I confess," I say to the bed, to the girls, to the vent, to the idea of a Board that will ask me to testify and then ignore every word. "I keep the ledger because someone must. I keep it so your numbers do not wander. I keep it so that when you die, you do not forget you were counted. I keep it so that when they say 'the poor in spirit are blessed' they will have proof they existed to be blessed."

The linen chute door unblisters. Metal cools. Ruthie stops clutching the mop like a rifle. The intercom clicks again and dies. The smell changes from silk to wet stone. It always does, after— the building chooses rain as its apology.

On the bed, under the ledger, there is a scorch in the shape of a bell. It is very neat. I will turn the mattress tomorrow and say nothing.

The girls need their Matron and I am still her. We finish our census with our throats like good ropes.

V. Legacy

02:55. The ward becomes itself again with the unshowy dignity of a woman refastening her hair. The radiators begin their little gossip; the lights stop presenting themselves. Somewhere in the north wing, the radio has found the right key. "Autumn Leaves" becomes "Abide with Me" as if October had changed its mind and become a hymn.

I write the last line of the ledger: **All present. Account at rest.** I add the hour. There is one name I do not add because it has added itself—mine—on the intake page for 13-C where no such page should exist. The letters curve with my hand's old vanity. I do not like seeing my vanity so plainly.

I return to my desk. The paper plan for M-13 has curled at the edges like a leaf on its way to ash. The signature *Carrow, Eng* is blurred into the fiber. I press the page flat and the page breathes. I put the bell on the plan's thin rectangle of hallway so the brass mouth covers the number. Mouth upon mouth. Silence upon rumor.

The tube chuffs. Another plan. The same plan. A new smudge. The hospital teaches you that repetition is not mistake but liturgy. You do the thing again not because it failed the first time, but because doing it is the point.

I think of the girls asleep upstairs after we change out. They will tell the day shift nothing because they will not remember *enough* to tell it right. The day shift will be grateful. It is a mercy to the day to let it believe it is the only shift.

I stand, and the chair remembers the shape of the person who sat there before me; for a second, the cushion is warm, and I am not in the room, and someone who thinks in lists is. When I step away, the chair forgets. This is the art the staff never learn and the reason I do not scold them when they cannot: to let a room forget you on purpose is a tenderness.

At three o'clock precisely, the chapel bell rings once, inside the vent and nowhere else. Not the tower bell—God forbid we touch that old throat. A small bell. A desk bell. The bell a nun or a clerk or a secretary uses to warn you she has seen you coming and is either pleased or not.

I pick up my pen. I sign the ledger page in my full name: **Margaret Hale, Matron.** I speak the policy line because it is mine and because speaking it makes the wall kinder: "Every number is a life, every life a record."

Behind the grate over my desk, the vent exhales. This one smells like starch and a candle blown close to the wick. In the duct, faint, someone writes in pencil. I hear it. It is a small sound like weaving. I am not alarmed. The sound is the sound of an institution instructing itself. The sound of a new hand practicing my loop on the capital H.

Tomorrow, there will be questions about a brief smoke alarm that did not sound, and a linen door that would not open and then would. There will be a Board memo with the exact right amount of sternness. They will say we must destroy any ledger pages that reference "events." I will applaud. I will put the papers in a box labeled **HVAC—Retired Parts,** and trust the building to file them where the living can find them when the numbers ask to be said aloud.

The girls will bring me coffee and a doughnut with orange frosting shaped like a leaf and I will pretend that sugar is nutrition. They will say they had the strangest dreams. One will dream her name written in red thread. One will dream she is standing in a hallway that does not exist and yet fits her feet as if it had memorized them. I will tell them that dreams are for people who sleep, not nurses, and we will laugh. We are good at laughing. It is another of the ward's disguises.

I close the book. The elastic leaves a welt on my thumb. Punctuation.

I place the bell atop the ledger and press it down so the brass mouth seals the ledger's last breath. In the duct, something sighs and a second bell—so faint I might be the only person alive who would hear it—rings in approval.

The light over the nurse's station flickers once. Twice. And steadies.

The door that is not a door where the linen closet has always been is a linen closet again. A row of sheets regards me, clean and folded and capable of any shape. I do not open the door to check the number. I do not need to.

At the end of my shift, when the sky has finally remembered how to be a window and the day staff are late by the predictable margin that keeps them human, I set the bell in my bag and feel it knock once against the ledger's spine. A companionship. A quiet animal asking to go home.

I lock my office. The lock is largely symbolic. Symbols teach more thoroughly than rules.

In the corridor, the vents make a sound like morning. A soft, hollow clatter—the steel bones of the old building stretching. Someone, somewhere, higher or lower than our maps allow, walks in time with my steps. One two three—pause—one.

On the way past the chapel I pause. Only the foolish enter a room that is perfectly still. I have never been a fool. I open the door anyway because I am a Matron.

On the altar there is a paper with my handwriting and not, both. *Census complete,* it says, and underneath, in a version of my hand I will not live long enough to own: *Account transferred. Steward: J.S.*

I touch the paper. It warms like a person with a fever. It refuses to cool even when I blow.

Outside, the bell in the tower declines to ring. Sensible tower. Inside the vent, a small bell rings once for courtesy.

"Present," I say to the empty chapel, because attendance is not for God, it is for buildings. It is for keeping the walls full of names to press against when they feel an ache where we were.

I leave the paper where it is. I do not erase the initials. I am not the beginning of the ledger and I am not the end. I am a page with good margins.

The day will come and take our night as if it were an empty tray. It will forget to say thank you. That is fine. Gratitude is for the petty. I am in the business of accounting.

At the nurse's station I sign out in a hand the Board will approve. I set the ledger in the bag and the bell on top and step into the stairwell that climbs a number of flights that are none of its own business.

At the landing between twelve and fourteen, there is a draft that smells like old milk and iron. I stand in it and it stands in me and then we are done.

When I open the door onto fourteen, the corridor is ordinary. It yawns. It wants a mop and a day nurse and the sound of slippers. It wants me to go to bed. I obey the ward the way the ward obeys me. We perform an old marriage—habit and mercy.

"Every number is a life," I say to the lamp over the exit, and the filament warms, and somewhere a pencil stops writing.

I go home before the building decides to count me twice.

— **M.H., Ward C Ledger, 03:15, October 31**

NOTE FROM JACK:

I found that file three nights ago—stuffed in the back of Records B behind a cabinet that shouldn't move and a drawer that definitely shouldn't open. The pages smelled like bleach and paper rot, but the handwriting was steady—Hale's.

I've read a lot of confessions down here, but this one wasn't meant for God or Warden. It was meant for *the building.*

There's something about the way she writes that makes the vents hum when you say her name out loud.

The Warden says the birthing floor's been sealed since '74.

Tonight, one of its lights came back on.

CHAPTER 1
THE NIGHT SHIFT BEGINS

JACK

Halloween. My favorite time of the year. You bet everything is decorated to the nines. I've got my skulls, my pumpkins, and all the best music blasting at all times.

Even on the floor. Well, it's not blasting, but you can bet it's playing from my office when I'm on shift.

If you don't know already, I love the Halloween shift, even when it's slow.

Especially when it's slow, it's the only night of the year when the building leans into what it really is—an asylum. There's an energy that pulses in the air, seeps right into the bones, and makes you feel alive in ways you didn't expect.

I understand that not everyone loves Halloween as much as I do, but if you've picked up this book, I think you share my enthusiasm for it.

The day-shifters all treat the place like a chore, like something someone else already half-finished, but on Halloween, the night staff knows better. We, on the night staff, understand the building best.

Ike and I came down to the break room. I was told it looks like a haunted house, so of course we had to come look. Whoever decorated down here gets an A+ for trying at least. It looks more like a morbid autopsy room covered in skulls and plastic pumpkins full of candy, but hey, at least they tried.

The break room is quiet. We're the only two in here. The vending machine hums like a tired choir, and my thermos sits between us, still steaming. I grind my own beans at home and brew them as dark as my mood and twice as strong. There's no way I'm drinking the garbage they make in this place. Whomever orders the supplies cheaps out on the coffee, that's for damn sure.

The lid unscrews with a soft sigh. As I pour, Ike eyes it like it I'm offering him a sip from the goblet of eternal youth.

I know how he feels.

Here's a thing about Ike that I appreciate. He has a way of holding the air still, like he's waiting for a punchline that's always on the tip of someone else's tongue. We sit together in silence long enough that I can hear the old clock in the hall, the kind with hands that scrape over invisible numbers. Everything about Ike is deliberate: the way he stacks his half-used sugar packets in a neat little row, the way his ID badge is always clipped dead-center, the way he wears his wedding ring like a trophy.

"You hear about Storage?" he asks, finally, tapping the table with a sugar packet he won't use. He doesn't look at me when he's nervous. He looks at habits.

I give him a side glance, see the furrow forming above his nose. "Storage is always noisy," I say, sliding him my spare enamel cup. "That's where we store noise."

Storage in this case is an actual noun.

He gives a single, hollow snort, takes a careful sip, and exhales. "Warden says keep it quiet."

"Warden says keep everything quiet. He'd whisper a fire alarm if he could."

Ike's eyes flick to mine, then back to the cup. He's been on nights almost as long as I have, and still lives the family dream, complete with a ring on his finger and texts from his wife at midnight asking if he's eaten. He's good at being a man who goes home in the morning and forgets what the building told him overnight.

I envy that. My own phone is a fossil, vibrating only when the system wants to remind me of a shift change or a new procedure for something we both know will never happen.

"Don't go up there alone," he says. There's something in his voice I can't quite put a pin in. What isn't he saying?

"There is no 'up there,'" I say. "We don't have a thirteenth floor." I don't even believe it, even though I've never found access to the floor. And trust me, I've looked.

He chuckles, then shakes his head. "Button jumps from twelve to fourteen, yeah. But the floor exists. It always does. You can pretend all you want that a number doesn't count, but I know better. I've been there."

Well, shit.

"Serious?"

He nods. "Rumor has it, access to it only happens on Halloween. What happens up there, stays up there, and you know better than to tell."

What the fuck?

"What are you talking about? What happened up there?"

He shakes his head. "Nope. Not a word. Just don't go up there. Trust me on this. Some floors are harmless. Some are ignored. Ours, it eats Halloween and spits out bells."

"Bells?"

"You'll hear it," he says, and I like that he says it like a promise. Nights like this feel wired. The air has edges.

I want to know more. He's been up there? Why is this the first I'm learning about it? But another thing about Ike, he's the kind who can keep secrets.

I pour myself another cup of coffee and try not to look at my own reflection. I'm not superstitious, but I've worked enough Halloween shifts to know when something is watching back.

"Last year," he says, low, like a confession, "I did rounds with Mona on Halloween. You remember her?"

I nod. Mona was a chain-smoker who could crack a dying joke to a cancer patient without breaking a sweat.

"We thought we heard a kid crying," he continues. "It was late, and you were hearing a story. We knew there was no one up there, but you know how it is, the way the walls bleed sound."

I nod again. There's a pressure in the room, like the walls don't want us to finish the story.

"We took the north stairwell to twelve, did a full sweep. Nothing. The crying continued." Ike sips, palm wrapped around the enamel cup like a handhold. "We did another sweep. Same. But by the time we made it back to the elevator, the crying was inside. Right behind the doors. Not a baby. Not a kid. Something old. Big."

He shrugs. "Mona quit two weeks later. Smelled like sulfur for days."

The vending machine cycles, humming and then grinding to a silent halt. I count the seconds between the old clock's clicks. The building moves around us, settling or remembering. I set my cup down and reach for my phone, but before I can check the time, it lights up: STORAGE DISTURBANCE. KEEP OFF LOG.

I turn the screen so Ike can see. His mouth sets in a hard line. "Of course." He folds his hands together, as if in prayer.

"You coming?" I ask.

He glances at the clock. Thinks about his rounds, about a patient who sleeps better when he reads her the med list like a lullaby. He shakes his head. "If it's nothing, text me a pumpkin emoji. If it's something—"

"—I text you a bell," I say.

He nods. "One ping."

"Sure." I cap the thermos, pocket my keys and bring up the recorder app on my phone. Warden might want this kept off record, but I've learned the hard way that I always need backup when it comes to him. I stand, stretch the tightness from my neck, and turn to the window. It's so dark out now that the glass is just a mirror. I can see Ike in it, smaller and farther away than he ought to be. I can see myself, or something close enough.

The night nurse trade is a kind of priesthood. You witness, you document, you pretend not to judge. But every hospital is really a church.

Every church is really a haunted house.

CHAPTER 2
THE ELEVATOR SKIPS 13

There are two ways to storage - the back stairwell, which everyone avoids, and the main elevators, which talk to you if you're listening.

I take the main elevators, but not before pausing in the hall for a second. The silence is never silent in this building, not really. Behind the moans and cries and the hum of lights, you can always hear the next thing, the thing that hasn't happened yet, getting ready.

Something is always about to happen, especially over Halloween.

The halls are lit by bulbs that have seen better decades. My footsteps sound wrong on the old tile—too measured, too echoing. I pass Room 108, the one they say was sealed after the fire, even though the fire never made it this far. The door is painted over, but sometimes the knob turns.

I don't look at it. I don't need that story tonight.

I round the corner and nearly collide with Del from security, who, as usual, is holding a clipboard and a flashlight that he uses more as a baton than a light source. "Admin wants you on storage?" he asks. Del is allergic to eye contact but not to rumors.

"Yeah," I say. "You see anything?"

He chews on his lip for a while. "I saw the elevator get stuck again. Doors stayed open for a whole minute." He pauses. "You know how it is."

He wants me to read between the lines, and I do.

"Yeah," I say, "I know how it is."

"New guy is coming up to escort you," Dixon says.

"What? Not you?" Not that I'm surprised. Why do a job if you can get someone else to do it for you? "I'll meet him up there. If I'm not back in twenty, call the Warden. And if you hear bells, you know the drill."

Dixon nods and disappears before I finish the sentence. I walk the last stretch to the elevator bay alone. The air pressure changes, like the building is breathing me in.

The doors stutter, then slide apart, and the lights inside are a little too white, like the color of teeth. I step in. The buttons stare back. Twelve. Fourteen. And between them, nothing. A literal absence. I press twelve.

The doors close with a sound like a coffin lid.

I take a breath, hit the record button, and speak into my phone. "Halloween shift, storage disturbance. I'm currently on floor Twelve. Apparently new guard is going to escort me." My voice sounds too loud. I lower the phone and hold it tight.

The elevator clatters to a stop. I expect the doors to wait, to make me sweat, but they slide open right away, like they're eager.

The lights are dim, and the air has a metallic taste. There's a smell, too, and I know it from busted freezers and spoiled meds: death, or something like it. I take a few steps, and the elevator dings behind me, but it doesn't close. I turn back, and it feels like a trap.

I text Ike a pumpkin. If I don't make it back, he'll know I tried to be funny.

Storage is a long, narrow corridor lined with cages containing expired equipment. Boxes and gurneys, pallets and mattresses. Most of it looks like it's been here longer than the staff. This place is exactly what you'd expect to find in a horror movie.

I walk past each cage, swinging my light and listening for anything but the rush of blood in my ears. The disturbance could be a dozen things. A loose rat. A busted vent. A ghost with some spare time.

At this hour, they all pay the same.

I reach the end of the corridor. The last cage is locked, but the lock is loose. I kneel to check it out. The pad is snapped, a clean break like it was made of candy. Someone broke it, but it's a security problem, not mine. The smell is more pungent here, and the cold hits different. I rub my hands together until the chill sets in my bones. "Nothing," I whisper to the recorder. "Texting a bell just in case."

I take a picture of the lock, send the emoji, and start the long walk back. Halfway, a sound like thunder or laughter shakes the ducts. I almost drop my phone, but the building knows better than to laugh at me. I slow my breathing, move on. Then I hear it. Crying, faint but close, like it's coming from the walls or from me.

I don't say a word. I just run.

You would too, so stop thinking I'm a chicken shit.

The elevator doors are still open when I reach them, holding their breath.

I leap inside, hit the button, hit it again for good measure.

The crying, it doesn't stop.

Someone has to be playing a prank on me.

CHAPTER 3
CRYING BEHIND THE WALLS

When the elevator's gears seize up at twelve, it's with the spastic jolt. Every time it happens, I think: this is it, we're stuck, and I'm going to be late to a haunting. But then the doors grind open just wide enough for a new layer of grime to join the others already welded to the lip of the threshold. The light in the hall is jaundiced, flickering overhead like the pulse of something sick, but at the far end is the new kid, hands in pocket, shuddering even though the air hasn't changed.

Name badge says Casper. First or last —no clue —but come on. Casper? Was his mother high or something? There are so many jokes I want to make but don't. The kid is fucking white, though, and I can't tell if it's from cold or fear.

Probably fear.

"You get stuck with the call, too?" He tries to play it like it's a joke, but that's just survival mode for him. He's got the prison-guard's humor, the kind that doesn't want to look anyone in the eye for too long.

"What did you do to get stuck on this?"

He pushes back his shoulders, like he's got something to prove.

"Calm down, kid. No one likes coming up here. So, either

9

you're new or you did something. I know how it works downstairs."

He glances at the elevator panel with its missing numbers, then back to me. "Didn't check all the storage doors last shift and didn't notice an inmate hiding inside it."

I snort. "Surprised you didn't get fired."

"Me too."

We move in tandem, like we're attached by a leash nobody sees. The corridor is a time capsule of failed sterilization, every surface slicked with residue that was once alive. Halfway down, there's an electrical box wedged into the wall at shin height.

The way the keys rattle in my hand is not nerves, it's just the hollow bones of the ring. I open the panel, and it exhales a little cloud of lint that's been aging in the dark.

Old places like this still get off on old keys. I fit the master in and twist. There's a click, and somewhere behind the walls, a switch slides into place.

The doors open and there's a moment, just a breath, where it feels like something has been waiting for us. We step in. The metal floor is cold through my shoes, colder than it should be, and I see Casper fight the urge to shiver.

He glances at the panel, then at me, then at the ceiling, as if the answer to why we're doing this might be written in cobwebs. "Where are we even going?"

"Wherever the call came from," I say. "You want to stay on twelve, get out now."

He doesn't. Honestly, I'm surprised.

The elevator lurches, and my stomach with it. The doors part on an in-between floor. The hallway is narrower, as if the concrete's been closing in slowly over the decades. There are a couple of derelict wheelchairs to the right, one overturned with its rubber wheels frozen in the air like a dead insect, the other sagging under the weight of a yellowed plastic bag that leaks slow, clear tears onto the floor.

"Jesus," the kid says, "what is this?"

He already knows, but everyone on this job needs to ask. It's a way of keeping the distance between what you see and what you want to remember.

I step out, and so does he, because elevators are never safe, and the first rule of the building is that the worst thing isn't what you find, it's what finds you.

"Why's it colder?" Casper whispers, hugging his arms.

"Because the building keeps its secrets in the dark," I say. "And it likes them fresh."

Am I joking? No.

I lead us to the next service panel, this one hidden behind a torn painting of a child holding an apple. The child's eyes follow us, one of them scratched out with something that left a rust-colored streak. I unlock the door and pull it wide, and there's that smell again, like old milk and ozone. The circuit box inside is painted black, a color so matte it eats the light.

I flip the topmost switch, and somewhere down the hall, a bulb flickers to life in a nurses' station window.

The nurses' station is a crescent of Plexiglas and Formica, post-apocalyptic in its emptiness. It has the feeling of a submarine, sealed off from the outside by years of neglect and resignation. I walk behind the counter and check the logbook. There's only one note, written in red ink:

IF YOU HEAR THE BELL, DO NOT ANSWER.

Well, fuuucckk. That's what Ike was talking about.

Casper looks over my shoulder to read the note, then quickly steps back.

"Too late to turn around," I warn him.

He swallows. Slowly.

The first ping is so sharp it carves the inside of my skull. I see Casper jump, his hand curling around a pen like he's going to stab whatever comes next. The sound is a frequency that's designed to bypass thought and go straight to the nerve.

"Did you hear—" Casper starts.

"I heard." I don't need to say more.

11

We follow the echo down a hall that's lined with ghost furniture. Gurneys with their straps undone, lamps with their shades pulled over their heads like prisoners waiting for last rites. At the end is a door labeled MATERNITY, the letters half peeled and rearranged over time until they spell something close to MARTYR.

Fuck. I forgot they had a maternity floor here. I'd heard rumors, but that was a long time ago.

I push the door and it gives, barely resisting, and the room beyond is a tableau of the uncanny: chairs arranged in a circle, each draped with a sheet that doesn't quite hide the shape beneath. At the center is a ring of salt, poured thick enough to suggest desperation, not ceremony. Four paper cups are placed at equidistant points, and in front of each is a spool of red thread, the line unspooling and running into a vent in the far corner.

Casper looks at me, his eyes saying what his mouth won't: This is not a drill.

The chairs are empty. But the sheets are not.

"Kids?" Casper asks, but he knows better.

"Kids don't make circles that tie wrists," I say. On the wall a nurse-call bulb blinks once and goes still. There's electrical tape over the switch. The power box in this wing shouldn't hum. But it does, faint, like a tune you almost recognize.

I kneel and lift the edge of one of the sheets. Underneath is a crude doll, made of surgical tape and gauze, its eyes two blackened pills, stitched in with a trembling hand. Every chair has one.

I replace the sheet and stand. Casper is at the vent, fingering the thread where it runs taut across the floor.

"Who does this?" he asks.

"You ever meet the inmates from the psych floor?"

He shakes his head. "They said we're not supposed to interact."

"That's because they know more about the building than we do."

He lets that sit for a second, then gestures at the circle. "The salt mean anything?"

"Depends who you ask," I say. "Some people think it keeps things in, some think it keeps things out."

He makes a sound halfway between a laugh and a shiver.

Outside the circle, the shadow of the door grows longer. It's not the light shifting, it's the dark moving in. I walk to the vent, which is propped open with a tongue depressor stained the same red as the logbook ink. The thread disappears inside, a vein waiting to be tapped.

There's a noise in the hallway, the rhythmic shuffle of feet that don't want to be heard.

Casper tenses. "We're not alone," he whispers.

No fucking shit.

CHAPTER 4
THE CONFESSION CIRCLE

They don't materialize out of nowhere, but they might as well have.

Pastor Cole and his cohort of three psychosomatic pilgrims shuffle their way into the spill of the nurses' station light like they've been waiting for the cue. They're not afraid of the dark. You can tell because it clings to them like old perfume, as if whatever they did before daylight was the only thing that mattered.

First is Cole: not tall, not broad, but when the overhead casts him across the wall, his shadow looks like a warning. He's got the kind of face that would score high with grandmothers and parole boards—thin lips, a stoic stretch of jaw, that small-town-choirboy thing. But there's a static charge to his eyes, something unblinking, as if sleep is a trick he's learned to do without. He grins, slow and loose, and the effect is less "welcome to church" and more "step into my office, let me show you the collection jar."

Close on his heels, half hidden, floats Nora Bell—bleached hair, skin pulled tight, the legacy of years spent trailing her own disaster. She fingers her palm constantly, rubbing at a scar or at nothing at all, and hovers near Cole with the loyalty of a dog that's been beaten just the right amount. She's dressed in the standard-issue blue, but she's made it her own: pants hiked up and knotted at the hip, shirt sleeves rolled so tight the seams bite into her arms.

Behind her, hands in pockets, is the other man, smaller, twitchier—Boone, I think his name is—who follows the others as if pulled by invisible magnets, always a step behind, always trembling with a suppressed something.

For a second, none of them says a word. Cole's smile widens, and he surveys the room like he's already run the simulation: salt ring, red thread, the dolls, the nurses' station with its blinking bulb. His face does not betray surprise.

"Brother Jack," he says, and the words are heavy with irony, though I don't know if he's mocking me or himself. "Welcome to our little revival." The accent is Midwestern, but somewhere along the way, he picked up a twist of something Southern, like the aftertaste of bourbon in a glass that's been washed out but never really cleaned.

I don't bother correcting him. Casper bristles, shifting his baton so it's visible, the way some people put their hand on a holstered gun when they think it makes them braver. "This floor's closed," Casper says, and you can tell he's working hard to sound like the only adult in the room, but the syllables tremble at the edge. "You're not supposed to be past ten. You're supposed to be in your dorm." The rules are all he has. He needs them to mean something.

Cole cocks his head, considering the statement like a question on a test he's already aced. "Everything worth hearing starts behind a closed door, don't you agree?" He gestures at the room, the circle, the chairs, and the doll beneath the sheet. "Besides, it's tradition. Matron always took her meals on twelve, no one else around. She would have liked the company." His eyes settle on the recorder at my hip, and then flick to the vent, and then back to me.

I keep my arms by my sides—no sudden moves—but I step forward so I'm blocking the salt circle with my body. "Circle's over," I say, and I mean it. "Whatever game you're playing, it stops now. We're walking back downstairs. Quietly." I shoot Casper a look that says, '*Do not fuck this up*'.

But Cole has no intention of turning back. He raises his bound wrist, where the red thread is cinched tight—a makeshift bracelet, the same as the one that tethers it to the wrist of the man next to him. Boone, now that I can see him better, is gray around the eyes and looks like he's been sweating out his nerves for hours.

"Give me ten minutes," Cole says, voice pitched low and reasonable, "and I'll give you a confession you can write down. Two men dead because I wanted them to see the light before they left it." He smiles again, and this time there's a flicker of self-loathing just under the surface. "No blades. No violence. Just talk."

It's a trap, it has to be. But I don't know for whom, and I don't know what kind.

Casper barks, "Bullshit," but his voice is reedy now. Not convincing anyone.

I glance at Nora Bell and the way she grips the spool of red thread in her hand, working it between her fingers like a rosary. She's watching Cole's every move, but her gaze keeps darting to the vent, the circle, the salt, as if she's afraid—or maybe hopeful—that something will intervene on their behalf.

"Three minutes," I offer, because sometimes the right lie buys time. "You so much as breathe wrong, we walk." I mean it. If it comes to it, the elevator is only twenty yards away. If I'm lucky, so is the fire alarm.

Cole nods, gracious in defeat, but I know it's just a stalling tactic. "Thank you for your patience," he says, and then he motions to the others with a tiny flick of his finger. They sit at the circle, not inside, not outside, but right on the line, like birds on a wire.

Cole kneels in front of the vent, presses his palm to the salt, and whispers something I don't catch. He's not praying, not exactly. If there's a God in this building, it's the kind that eats prayers for breakfast and washes them down with bleach.

"Matron Hale," Cole says, his voice gentle as a lullaby, "we call you to witness." It's not a command, not a request. More like a promise. Or an apology.

And then the nurse-call bulb flares—once, twice—like it's a living thing that just woke up angry.

Casper swears, steps backward. "Holy shit, holy shit, holy shit."

I lean on the recorder with my thumb, already feeling the tape spin.

And then we all hear it: from inside the vent, a woman's voice, so soft it could be the wind, but not the way wind sounds. It's the way words sound when you're about to cry, or when you realize you've been alone in the house for hours and the phone is dead.

"Ephraim," it says. The syllables float on a breath that feels cold and wet, like the air from a freezer. "You always liked a show."

Cole doesn't move. His eyes flick up, but he doesn't blink. For the first time, there's no smile.

Something electric jumps across the room. I watch as Nora Bell's hands knot tighter around the thread, her knuckles whitening with the force of it. Boone actually whimpers, a high-pitched, involuntary sound, and now I'm not sure if he's afraid of Cole or the thing in the vent.

I look at Diaz and see his eyes go wide. He'll see plenty of shit on this job if he sticks to it—suicides, fights, people eating their own tongues—but whatever is happening now is outside the usual catalog, and I doubt they covered this in orientation.

It's not ghosts, not exactly, but it's something that makes the bones in your wrists ache.

No one moves for a long moment.

All eyes go to Cole because everyone wants to know if the next step is his or if he's lost control entirely.

CHAPTER 5
SECURITY INCIDENT REPORT – STORAGE DISTURBANCE

(Filed: October 29, 1996 | Location: North Wing, Sublevel B – Restricted Storage)
    (Recovered and reclassified by Nurse J. Steen, Graveyard Shift)

Report Summary
    Reporting Officer: Guard T. Hargreaves
    Supervisor on Duty: C. Holt (Warden)
    Incident Type: Unauthorized Access / Mechanical Anomaly
    Time Logged: 02:03–02:47 A.M.
    Witnesses: Custodian M. Gasper, Nurse I. Talbot
    Status: Unresolved

Incident Narrative
    At approximately 02:03 A.M., night monitor detected movement in corridor camera 12B (Storage Access). Video feed showed distortion, static interference, and a brief silhouette of unknown personnel near the locked gate.

    Guard Hargreaves dispatched for inspection.

    Upon arrival, corridor appeared unoccupied. Door to Storage

B secured but handle was *warm to touch* (approx. 45°C per thermal reader). No visible fire or heat source. Custodian Gasper confirmed HVAC fans offline at the time.

Nurse Talbot arrived to verify medication logs and stated she heard *"soft humming through the vent, like a lullaby or prayer."*

Audio feed corroborates low-frequency tonal pattern (rhythmic, three beats, one pause, repeating). Pattern continued for 38 seconds before ceasing.

Storage B lock mechanism found *partially melted* yet intact.

Warden Holt authorized cutting torch entry at 02:41 A.M.

Inside, the room was *empty*—no contraband, no personnel. However, all stacked cardboard boxes were now labeled in fresh marker: **"ACCOUNT CLOSED."**

Each label written in identical cursive.

No fingerprints recovered.

Incident concluded at 02:47 A.M.

Additional Observations

- Infrared sweep recorded temperature differential: localized *cold spot* (-4°C) above vent shaft.
- Technician reported metallic ringing echoing from inside ductwork after inspection.
- Floor tiles beneath vent show hairline cracks forming concentric circles—three full rings.

Supervisor's Closing Remarks (Warden Holt)

"Security breach dismissed as electrical interference from ventilation wiring. Repaint tiles, reseal duct, and remove any boxes with the phrase *'Account Closed.'*

Recommend personnel avoid mythologizing isolated mechanical faults.

Official reminder: There is no thirteenth floor."
Signed,
C.V. Holt
Warden

[Addendum – Unofficial Entry, Date Unknown]
(Handwriting believed to be that of Custodian M. Gasper)
Repainted tiles, yes. But cracks came back overnight. Three rings again, only closer together. Looks like the floor's breathing. If anyone else finds boxes down here, don't touch the ink. It's still wet.

[Margin Notes – J. Steen]
First mention of the phrase "Account Closed." Appears again in Cole's confession ledger, fifty years later.

The handwriting sample matches the Matron's recovered personnel file.

Either someone forged it... or she's still doing inventory.

Note to self: pull the 1996 maintenance shift roster. Find out if Gasper's still alive.

I close the file and sit back in the chair, listening to the hum of the vents above my head. It's faint, but the rhythm's the same—three beats and a pause. The kind of sound you can almost mistake for your own heartbeat if you sit still long enough.

I tell myself it's just bad wiring. Then I hear the whisper: *account closed.*

Guess the building keeps better records than I do.

CHAPTER 6
HANDS TELL THE TRUTH

I've learned to watch the hands. Mouths lie because mouths are made for it. Hands remember truth because they've done the work. Cole's hands are careful—prison hands that learned to be still so they wouldn't be a reason to get hit. But when the voice says his given name, his fingers flex against the red thread like a man remembering he's tied to something.

"You know me," Cole says to the vent, but the sentence sounds like he's asking permission.

"Everyone knows you," the woman says. There's a click behind her words, a relay tick, the sound of a building clearing its throat. "You baptize fear and call it faith."

He recovers fast, because con men are athletes. "We're telling the truth tonight."

"You first," the voice says.

He looks at me. "Recorder on?"

"It's on," I say. My thumb is steady. My heart isn't.

"Two men," Cole begins, and for a moment I forget the vent and the bulb and the circle that isn't salt, because storytelling is a drug and he's a practiced dealer. "Halloween lockup, county jail. Worship night that wasn't about worship. We sang. I prayed. I dosed. They saw a light. Two didn't come back. I told myself it was my job to walk them to the edge. Only God decides who steps over." He breathes. "I believed that until I didn't."

The voice in the wall hums like someone nodding.

"Write down their names," it says. "Say them like you mean them."

Cole does. He says a last name I've seen before, attached to a transfer that didn't transfer. He says another that tastes like a lawsuit the county settled fast. His voice thins on the second syllable. He looks older when fear remembers him.

"Why here?" I ask, because the recorder needs a spine. "Why this floor?"

Cole's eyes flick to the vent. "Because this is where she learned it first."

"She?" Diaz asks.

"Matron Hale," Cole says, and the bulb flares like the name is a match. "Head nurse who taught men to breathe through pain like it was a privilege. Every miracle has a price. She tallied hers in a ledger that went missing and a floor that got sealed because paperwork got tired."

"You believe that," I say.

He nods. "Belief is a habit. I try to keep mine from killing people."

"Not a great batting average," I say.

He smiles with half his mouth. "You going to let me finish?"

"Three minutes are up," I say, as the bulb finally goes dark. I stand, step over the crooked circle, and reach for the red thread where it enters the vent. It tugs back like a fish testing line. I look at Cole. He doesn't move.

"Don't," Nora Bell says. It's not fear in her voice. It's possession. "If you break it, she stops talking."

"If she's a ghost," I say, "she's not afraid of broken thread."

I pinch and pull. The thread slides through the vent smooth as a lie, unspooling from somewhere I can't see. It keeps coming, longer than it should be. Somewhere inside the wall, something knocks three times and then the thread goes slack in my hand all at once like whoever was holding the other end let go.

The vent sighs words again, faint, clipped, careful: "Leave my floor."

The elevator down the hall coughs, a relay snapping. The recorder clicks on my palm like it has opinions. Cole lowers his head. Diaz takes a step back. Nora smiles the way magpies smile when they've seen something shiny.

I pocket the thread like a receipt. "Circle's over," I say. "We're leaving. We'll talk downstairs."

"Brother Jack," Cole says, eyes still down, "if we go now, she'll follow you."

"I'm not a church," I say. "I'm a night nurse."

He looks up. "That's closer than you think."

I hate when they're right.

We walk them back toward the elevator, red thread trailing out of the vent like a vein someone cut and forgot to tie off. The bulb doesn't blink again. The building breathes, and for a second I swear I hear a voice say my name, not from the vent but from the small panel in the hallway wall where the pneumatic tubes used to run like arteries.

The elevator doors open like a yawn turned into a warning. We step inside. Diaz exhales.

On our way down, Cole says, almost conversational, like we're discussing weather, "You ever wonder why the Warden keeps this off the books?"

"Every day," I say.

"Because some ghosts are alive."

He smiles when he says it, but it doesn't reach his eyes.

I can still feel it—the pulse beneath the skin, the tremor before truth rises.

My hands are clean now. At least, that's what I tell myself when the lights go out and the air presses back.

Somewhere in the walls, something stirs—slow, deliberate, like a heart that's learned how to lie.

I close my eyes and let it speak.

CHAPTER 7
PLAYBACK

JACK

The vent hums again—steady this time, like it's learning a heartbeat.

I keep my thumb on the recorder. Static fills the room, white and clean, a sound you could almost mistake for silence.

Here's a trick I've picked up in my years on the graveyard shift: if you want the truth, don't watch a person's face. Faces lie for a living. Watch the hands.

Cole's are the kind you only find in ex-cons and magicians. Still out of habit, but not at peace. The red thread cuts across his fingers like a warning, the knuckles tight, joints strung for impact.

Then the voice—her voice—slides out of the vent. It says his name.

His hands betray him before his mouth does.

Just now, he's got his fingers wound with the red cord like he's bracing for a current, knuckles white, tension in each joint. Still, but not steady. Not really used to being still. He's ready to strike or surrender, whichever comes first.

So when the voice—her voice—says Cole's actual Christian

name out the vent, his hands betray him. The thread quivers, the fingers flex, like an inmate remembering the taste of cold cuffs. He collects himself, but by then it's too late. He makes eye contact with me and tries to act casual, but the mask is cracked.

"You know me," he says, talking to the wall, but the way he says it, I half expect him to drop down on his knees and beg.

The voice doesn't miss a beat. "Everyone knows you, Mr. Cole," it says, the syllables ticked and precise, like a nurse counting pills. "You baptize fear and call it faith."

That line is good—so good it nearly throws me. Cole recovers faster. He's a pro, a lifer in the con game, and the words don't rattle him for long. "We're here for truth tonight," he says, and it sounds like he's selling tickets.

"Then begin," the voice returns, and now it's fluttery, almost bored. I wonder if she's done this a thousand times—maybe she has. I hit record on the phone. My thumb is the only thing steady in the room, because if I stop moving, my heart will climb out my throat.

Cole glances at me, the question plain as a billboard. I nod. He starts.

"Two men," he says, rolling it like a coin between his teeth. "Halloween lockup, county jail. Said it was a worship night, but we knew it was a set-up. They wanted a group to test the new system, see if it'd break us or break the ghosts. We sang. I prayed." His mouth twitches. "I dosed. They saw a light. Two didn't come back."

He lets the words hang, like he's waiting for applause. I know the story, but I don't know the twist until he says, "I told myself my job was to walk them to the edge. Only God decides who steps over." He inhales, deep and cautious, like the air might cut him if he breathes too hard. "I believed that until I didn't."

The woman in the duct hums, a sound like a piano string plucked deep in the hull of the hospital.

"Write down their names," she says. "Say them like you mean them."

Cole pulls a slip of receipt paper from his jacket and scribbles fast. He reads. The names come out jagged, last names first, the way they do on intake forms.

One I recognize—a transfer that never showed up. County lost the paperwork. Another name tastes like a lawsuit, the kind nobody talks about but everyone remembers. His voice is gone by the end, hollowed out. I think I see him age a year in three seconds. Fear is a tax. It collects fast when it's backlogged.

Nora Bell, sitting opposite him, leans in, chin propped on her palm. Her smile belongs on an animal that knows it's already won.

I ask the question the recorder needs: "Why here? Why this floor?"

Cole swallows. Glances at the vent. "Because this is where she learned it first."

"She?" Diaz says, eyes wide, as if she's not sure if she's the audience or next on the list.

"Matron Hale," Cole says. The bulb above us goes migraine-bright for a split second, then settles back, like the name is its own incantation. "She ran the night ward. Believed pain was a teacher. If you lived, you learned. If you didn't, you were a lesson. They say she kept a ledger—wrote it all down—the number of breaths, the number of screams. Ledger went missing. So did the matron. They sealed this floor because they didn't want her brand of education getting out."

"You actually believe that?"

Cole nods, shame-faced. "Belief is a muscle. You use it, or it atrophies. I try to keep mine from killing people."

"Not a great batting average," I say.

He shrugs, half a laugh. "You want me to finish this, or are we doing commentary?"

I check the timer. "Three minutes. We're done here." The bulb throbs a final time, then dies. I get up, feeling the gravity in my knees, and step over the chalky line of the almost-salt circle. The red thread runs from Cole's hand to the vent, and I follow it, reach for the slack where it enters the wall.

It tugs back, sharp, like something on the other side is fighting for it. I glance at Cole. He's not blinking.

Nora cuts in, cold as ever: "Don't pull. If you break it, she stops talking."

I hear the implication: She stops talking, but not listening.

"If she's a ghost, she'll find another way," I say, but my hand is already on the cord, pinching it. It slides through my fingers, smooth as a snake.

This is the part no one warns you about: the lengths. The red thread keeps coming, more and more, yards of it, like the hospital itself is unraveling. Somewhere inside the wall, something knocks. Three times. A warning or an invitation. And then the thread goes limp, like a dead limb. Nothing fights me on the last pull.

Behind us, the vent sighs again, a whisper this time, clipped and careful: "Leave my floor."

Down the hall, the elevator rattles, a mechanical bark. My phone shudders in my pocket, the recorder flipping itself off and on. I can't tell if it's glitching or trying to get my attention. Cole stares at the ground, hands empty. Diaz edges back. Nora stands, smoothing her skirt, and grins like a crow.

I coil the thread, pocket it. "Circle's over," I tell them. "We leave. Nobody looks back. We talk downstairs."

Cole's voice is quieter than I've ever heard it. "Brother Jack—" And there's something sorrowful in it, like he's about to confess. "If we go now, she'll follow you."

I smirk, but it tastes like rust. "I'm not a church. I'm a night nurse."

He lifts his eyes. "That's closer than you think."

I hate it when I agree with him.

We walk down the hall, single file, like a funeral without a body. The red thread snakes from the vent, trailing after us, a vein that refuses to clot. The bulb at the end of the corridor is dark, but the building still breathes. I hear my name hissed, not from the vent but from the pneumatic tube panel by the fire door—like the old system is still running messages. Maybe it is.

The elevator doors open slow, but no one walks in.

"A deal is a deal," Cole says. "I owe you a confession."

I nod and wonder where he's going with this.

"We'll head back to our unit. You go to your floor. Meet me in the chapel after lights out. I'll tell you the rest."

Casper looks confused, but I lightly push him into the elevator and then hold the doors open with my hands as I watch the others turn around and leave.

The red cord in my pocket burns cold on my skin, but I don't take it out.

Casper is the first to break the silence. "You hear that?" he says.

I hear it: a song, half hummed, half screamed, leaking out from the elevator shaft. It's the melody from upstairs—the same song.

Fucking storage, I mutter. This isn't going to go well, I can already feel it.

CHAPTER 8
THE NIGHT THE CHAPEL WAITED

The elevator hums like it's nursing a grudge all the way back to my death floor. The overheads are always a little dimmer than regulation, the walls a touch too gray, like the ghosts of old disinfectant stains can't be scrubbed out. The ride is long enough for me to notice the blinking camera in the corner, its little cyclops eye recording my face, and I give it the finger just to see if Security's watching.

They are. I know, because the next floor, the doors stick and then jerk open, catching on something, and I swear I can hear giggling down the line.

There's a familiar stink of antiseptic and half-forgotten meals as I step out of the elevator. They say every hospital smells the same, but this one's bouquet is uniquely aggressive. Imagine a chemical weapons lab staffed entirely by cafeteria rejects, and you're getting there.

From somewhere down the hall, a wet cough escalates into a scream, then back to coughing. Probably Franklin in 319 again—he's been dying for months, and he's not shy about sharing the process.

Home, if hell ever needed an address.

Ike's leaning against the med cart, rolling his shoulder like a pitcher warming up before the ninth inning. He's got a coffee in one hand, a clipboard in the other, and a thin, dangerous smile like he's heard every joke and can name which ones are funny. He glances up as I step out, and his eyes do a full-body scan, reading the story on my face before I can even think about lying.

"Let me guess," he says, not bothering to lower his voice even with the hallway traffic. "Another miracle gone sideways."

I let the words hang there, watching the scrubs and orderlies hustle by, their faces locked in that tight, exhausted beam that says don't make eye contact and maybe you'll live through the shift. Someone's spilled something rainbow-bright on the linoleum, and a janitor with stiff joints is mopping it like he's painting a masterpiece in slow motion.

"Depends what you call a miracle," I answer.

Ike lifts the thermos and pours me a mug, the steam curling up like a spirit fleeing the scene. He holds it out, pinky extended, and I take it, nodding my thanks.

He leans in, dropping his voice a notch, as if the building itself might be eavesdropping. "You find him?"

"Found him. Found something else, too."

He arches an eyebrow. "The kind of something that'll make the Warden twitch or the kind that'll get us reassigned to laundry?"

I take a big sip, instantly regretting it as the coffee scalds my tongue. I grin anyway, because pain and caffeine are the only things keeping me vertical. "Both."

He whistles low, a sound that always makes me think of broken bones and bad news. "Damn it, Jack."

I shrug, looking past him to the plexiglass window at the end of the corridor where a moth the size of my palm is battering itself senseless against the glass, leaving a ghostly dust trail with every assault. "The chapel," I say, "I'm headed there for story time."

Something in Ike's face changes, like a light going out behind his eyes. He lowers his mug, sets it on the cart, and stares at me over the rim of his clipboard. "Pastor Cole?"

I nod. "He offered a story. I said yes."

He glances up and down the hallway, then leans in again. "You know it's not just him, right? The stories, the—whatever they are. The new guy in 327, the one who tried to off himself with the rosary beads? He's been talking about the chapel, too. Sees things. Hears things. Said last night the walls were bleeding."

"Walls don't bleed," I say, which is a lie—I've seen them do worse. I sip again, more slowly this time.

Ike shakes his head. "You ever think maybe there's a reason the old priest hung himself in there? Maybe he saw what was coming."

"You believe Cole?" I ask, genuinely curious. "You think he's —the real thing?"

Ike rubs his jaw, the stubble sandpaper-rough. "I think anyone locked in here long enough gets hungry for meaning. Doesn't matter what flavor. Methodists? They just get weepy. Catholics? They get haunted. But Cole? He was different before they brought him in. Didn't see ghosts. Didn't hear voices. Now…" He shrugs, hands up. "Now he's got you sneaking around after midnight."

"It's Halloween," I say, trying for a joke. "Everyone talks to the dead tonight."

He doesn't laugh. Instead, he bites his lip, and for a second, I think he's about to tell me to drop it, but he just looks tired. "Jack," he says finally, "if the building starts talking again—don't answer."

I want to promise, but the words get stuck in my throat, thick and heavy as blood. Instead, I drain the mug and hand it back to him, the dregs swirling like an omen. "If I'm not back by sunrise, check the boiler room. I'll be the one wearing a halo."

Ike rolls his eyes, but there's a flicker of worry in his grin. "You're not funny, Steen."

I spread my hands. "I'm trying. Maybe I'll work on my material in purgatory."

He snorts. "If you're late, I'm stealing your snacks."

We stand there, facing each other over the gulf of a thousand unspoken things. The hallway is empty now, the clock on the wall ticking so loud it sounds like a threat. My shift is half over, but I already know the night is just getting started.

I grab my recorder, slip it into my pocket, and head for the chapel. The lights flicker once, twice, and hold. The building knows I'm coming.

CHAPTER 9

BOARD TRANSCRIPT – COLE DISMISSAL HEARING

By now, you are aware that Cole is a patient, an inmate, and not the staff chaplain, although my understanding is they certainly allow him leniencies down on the isolation floor. I believe this 'transcript' was planted by Ike as a prank.

BOARD TRANSCRIPT - Confidential Proceedings of the Disciplinary Board

(Recovered and Annotated by Nurse J. Steen) with a note: Ephraim Cole has always been a patient in this asylum, never the staff chaplain. This is obviously a prank and I bet it's by Ike)

Attendance

- **Dr. Harold Venn** – Chairman
- **Warden Charles V. Holt** – Administrative Observer
- **Dr. Ephraim Cole** – Staff Chaplain (Respondent)
- **Recorder:** E. Winslow, Stenography Dept.
- **Observer:** Matron M. Hale (absent – presumed deceased)

. . .

Opening Statement

Venn: This hearing convenes to address allegations of theological misconduct, falsification of patient records, and unauthorized nocturnal assemblies in Ward C. Reverend Dr. Cole, you've been observed leading gatherings inconsistent with hospital policy and clinical ethics.

Cole: Gatherings? You make them sound festive. They were services of restoration.

Venn: Patients were harmed. One died.

Cole: No—*balanced.*

Holt: (Interrupts) Doctor, please restrict yourself to medical language.

Cole: Medicine and faith speak the same tongue, Warden. You just pretend you don't understand the dialect.

(Pause. Chairman clears throat.)

Excerpt 1

Venn: Explain this entry found in your personal log: *"Three for the living, one for the lost."*

Cole: It's a measurement. Every healing takes three breaths, one offering. The same ratio your heart keeps if you listen close enough.

Holt: Is that numerology or superstition?

Cole: Arithmetic. The Lord's original math.

Venn: And the phrase *"ledger due"* — does that appear in any recognized scripture?

Cole: Only the one written between your ribs.

(Recorder notes: Extended silence – unidentified knocking picked up on tape, four beats.)

Excerpt 2 – Cross-Examination

Holt: You admit to bloodletting rituals with patients.

Cole: "Bloodletting" makes it sound wasteful. It's an exchange. Every cure needs a currency.

Holt: And who authorizes this "currency"?

Cole: The Matron. Same as you, Warden—only she still does rounds.

(Chairman asks that record reflect subject's tone: calm, smiling.)

Venn: Matron Hale is dead, Dr. Cole.

Cole: Then why did she sign the attendance sheet last night?

(Paper shuffle. Recorder notes rustling, faint bell ring.)

Excerpt 3 – Recommendation for Dismissal

Venn: Given the evidence — unauthorized liturgies, symbolic mutilations, patient fatalities — this Board recommends immediate termination and transfer to psychiatric evaluation.

Holt: I'll arrange transport to the State Unit by dawn. Burn everything he wrote.

Cole: You'll never balance the books without me.

(Recorder notes final remark delivered in whisper. When played back, voice duplicated in echo approximately 0.7 seconds delay.)

Administrative Summary (Appended August 3, 1958)

Dr. Ephraim Cole released to state custody.

All materials referencing *The Ledger Program* sealed.

Internal audit found unauthorized duplication of Hale patient files. Source unidentified.

Board advises staff to disregard rumors of "the bell in the vents."

Signed,

H. Venn, Chairman

C.V. Holt, Warden

. . .

[Margin Notes – J. Steen, 2025]

- First written evidence connecting Hale and Cole directly.
- The *echo* on the tape matches modern audio interference near the chapel microphone—0.7 seconds exactly.
- Holt's order to *burn everything* explains why half our archives smell like candle wax when the vents warm up.

I wonder if the "balance" he mentioned wasn't spiritual but administrative. Someone's still keeping ledgers, and the accounts never close.

— J.S.

The transcript ends mid-sentence, a hiss of tape that never quite resolves. The silence after is worse than any scream—it sounds like waiting.

I flip the page and see my own initials typed at the bottom of the scan header. J.S.

Yep, this is definitely a prank because I sure as hell didn't add my initials to this.

CHAPTER 10
THE MAKING OF A MIRACLE

EPHRAIM COLE

People tend to picture miracles as if they're wrapped gifts, just waiting for someone to lift the bow and find salvation inside. I learned early on that real miracles don't drop like presents. You build them yourself—hammering out the shape, polishing the edge, and then slipping that sharpened truth into somebody else's hand like a blade of grace.

The first one nearly slipped through my fingers.

I was nineteen, locked in a county jail cell so narrow that every breath felt borrowed. Hunger gnawed at me, deeper than any skipped meal could account for, rattling through my bones like a warning bell. The chaplain, a wiry man with hollow eyes, shuffled through the tiers, dragging a battered guitar with only two strings.

On Halloween night, he gathered us beneath the harsh glare of fluorescent bulbs, their buzzing hum a fake thunder. He led off-key hymns—each note lurching and cracking—while he flung handfuls of candy across the concrete like scraps of mercy. The guards peered through thick plexiglass windows, our faces distorted, like fish staring at some unknowable fisherman's boat.

There was a kid on my floor that everyone called Looper. He'd been born without a compass needle in his chest, always spinning, always searching for somebody to tell him which way was north. His loyalty was a hunger; he would have branded himself just to taste the burn of purpose. His eyes were the pale, washed-out blue you see in photo booth pictures that were left too long in sunlight. He clung to me because I spoke softly, asked simple questions he could nod "yes" to, and in my quiet voice, he heard something like direction.

That night, during 'Amazing Grace', I filched a powder from the med cart. Just enough to wake a heart that'd gone numb, if you know what I mean. I stirred it into a cup of the jail's stale coffee, where the grounds floated like drowned secrets.

Handing it to Looper, I shrugged and said, "This'll help the nerves." He swallowed it with the kind of trust that only a boy with nothing else to believe in can muster.

Twenty minutes passed slow as eternity. Then his skin began to deepen, shifting toward the drab gray of the concrete below him. His chest trembled once and stopped.

The room lurched awake, the emergency siren flaring—half furious, half weary, like it hadn't been called on in a hundred lifetimes. Men scrambled, tripped over benches, spilled into each other, coughing up fear in frantic choreography.

But Looper's eyes stayed open, impossibly wide. In their reflection, I saw a corridor stretching beyond the bars, beyond the flicker of broken lights, into someplace I had never dared to look.

When he came back, the fear had drained out of him, left him hollow but fearless. I realized then that fear is a currency—only worth something if someone chooses to mint it, stamp it, spend it. He'd spent his all, and owed no more.

The chaplain knelt beside him later, weeping into his collar, calling it an attack by some unholy spirit, a warning they'd failed to heed.

I smiled, told him it was a sign of something bigger. He straightened up like a child relieved to know God was in the front row, applauding.

By dawn, guys were pressing against my cell door, begging me for the same shock. They wanted me to press my hands across their shoulders, as if my skin could channel lightning.

I taught myself to draw breath slow and low, to string words that felt too wide for that little room, to pose questions with only yes-or-no answers that split open the ribs of secrets.

I watched the air grow charged, watched the knees buckle under anticipation. I learned how belief moves through a crowd— like a draft drifting through open windows—tender to the bodies already bowed.

A draft can shape a miracle. Tie a red thread to it, and people start swearing you're in direct line to the divine.

Miracle number two was cold-blooded calculation. I'm not proud, I admit it, but the truth hurts less than the lie. We had another kid, Choir, who would stand by the vent each night and bawl out tunes he couldn't carry a melody through. He said he was singing "to the other side," as if it were a neighbor's apartment he hoped might answer.

I took two paper cups, pricked pinholes at their bases with my thumbnail, ran a spool of red thread through them, knotting it under the table. I told the men to sit cross-legged around me, each with a fingertip resting on a cup. "No pushing," I warned. "Let the confession do the work."

Desire drives the cups upward; guilt keeps them trembling. But the real trick was the thread, wrapped around my hand under the tabletop, snaking through a vent loose from its screws.

On the other end, Choir held a kite reel I'd stolen from intake. Three tugs from me, one from him, and the cups slid across the table as if buoyed by faith. The men gasped, the guards froze, and in that hush we called it communion without wine.

Halloween in here always felt tattered, as if the masks people wore were half the set design. The ugly fluorescent lights cast long, jagged shadows that turned the cells into cathedrals of panic. Men crave the tremor of terror—so that they can suck in the relief of not being dead.

Relief, I decided, is stronger than morphine and more elusive than any drug test can ever catch.

Two years later, I set my sights on a spectacle: a mass revival of the damned.

Two men dosed together, meant to rise as prophets. Looper made it back. Choir didn't.

Parnell—our second volunteer—was buried beside him.

I tried to baptize their deaths into a sermon, told anyone who'd listen that God hand-picked two souls to go home early.

Some nights I whispered that and almost believed it.

Most nights I only heard the thread slipping through a hollow knot.

CHAPTER 11
THE SERMON OF BLOOD

NOTE FROM JACK:

There are sermons that save and sermons that stain. Cole's was the second kind.

The Warden asked me to record it, said it was evidence. But it didn't feel like evidence—it felt like an invitation.

He called it *A Sermon of Blood*.

I'm including it here because pretending I didn't hear it hasn't stopped it from playing in my mind.

They always think a sermon begins at the pulpit.

But the first sermon begins the moment a man decides he's been heard by something that shouldn't be listening.

The first time *I* was heard, I was twelve.

My father kept the slaughterhouse behind our house, out past the hedge where the air smelled like old coins and salt. He said animals were God's arithmetic—every bleat a subtraction, every heartbeat a tally toward supper. He wasn't cruel. Just devout in the wrong direction.

He used to test me. "You think you know scripture, boy?" he'd say, wiping his knife on a rag. "Show me the verse where God says mercy is free."

I never could.

Because it isn't.

I learned the price one autumn afternoon when the generator failed mid-slaughter. The lamb kicked, the knife slipped, and I felt its blood slick my wrist—warm, metallic, forgiving. I pressed my hand to the wound to stop the life from leaving, and for one suspended breath, I swear I felt the blood *pulse back* like it recognized me. Like it was saying, *not yet.*

That was my first miracle. My father called it blasphemy.

He made me kneel in the shed all night, hands clasped, reciting Psalm 51 until my throat turned raw: *Wash me, and I shall be whiter than snow.*

By morning, the lamb was gone. So was the guilt.

But when I looked at my hands, I saw the stain beneath the skin, like something had moved in.

The next miracle came ten years later.

I was preaching to a congregation that didn't want saving—factory men, whiskey breath, wives too tired to care. A pastor's inheritance.

That night, during the hymn, the old man who sat in the front pew—Mr. Talbert, seventy-eight, widower, heart trouble—collapsed. The choir stopped mid-verse. I was the first to reach him. I remember the smell of varnish, sweat, and fear.

He was gone.

But the congregation was watching, needing a sign.

And I wanted—oh, I *wanted*—to give it to them.

So I laid my palm on his chest and whispered the same rhythm that had come to me that night in the shed. Not words, exactly—just a pulse, three beats and a pause. A blood psalm.

And Mr. Talbert opened his eyes.

He gasped. Sat up. Called my name.

The room broke open with hallelujahs.

It should have been joy.

But there was something off in his gaze—something black, deep in the pupil, like a coin dropped down a well.

The next morning he was dead again. Only this time he'd bitten through his own tongue. I heard he died smiling.

That was the moment I understood: resurrection and rot share the same hymn if you sing it loud enough.

Word spread. *The miracle preacher.*

People came from counties away. They filled the pews with their sickness—arthritis, consumption, despair. They wanted me to touch them. To bless them. To barter with God on their behalf.

And I did.

And each time, someone else got sicker.

A child healed; her mother miscarried.

A drunk walked straight; a stranger drowned the next day in a ditch behind the bar.

The ledger balanced itself, always.

I started keeping records—names, dates, symptoms. I wanted to understand the math. Maybe I could learn to control it.

That's when I found the red ledger.

It was in the church basement, hidden behind the baptismal font. Wrapped in a waxed cloth and bound with a cord so tight it had cut into the leather. When I opened it, the first page read simply:

"All accounts must reconcile in blood."

There were names inside. Old ones.

Dates going back a century.

Every few pages, a symbol—a bell, a thread, a pair of hands crossed at the wrist. I thought it was the work of mad monks or bored deacons.

But the book *breathed*. The pages would ripple when I spoke certain verses. The ink would bleed forward, forming words I hadn't written.

It spoke in ledgers, in balance sheets, in pulse counts.

And I listened.

The miracles changed after that.

Sharper. Cleaner. Predictable.

When I cut my palm, I could feel it listening, waiting to collect. When I bled into the chalice during communion—just a drop— half the congregation fainted, the other half wept.

We started Sunday service at midnight. The faithful called it "The Red Hour."

They said the Holy Spirit visited through me.

They weren't wrong.

The night the bishop came to investigate, I prepared a special demonstration.

He didn't believe in my ledger or my psalm.

So I showed him.

I brought out a volunteer, one of the mill boys who'd been born with a twisted spine.

I asked the congregation to pray. They did.

And I read from the ledger.

The boy screamed, then straightened, bones cracking like branches thawing in spring. The bishop fell to his knees. "It's a miracle," he whispered.

But I saw what no one else did—the shadow of the boy's spine standing behind him, still bent, still twitching. It lingered for three full seconds before the light swallowed it whole.

Balance.

The next morning, the bishop's carriage derailed on the way home. They said the horses bolted.

I said *Amen.*

After that, the Church excommunicated me.

They said I was a sorcerer, not a shepherd.

Maybe they were right.

Because sorcery is just faith without permission.

They dragged me away mid-sermon, wrists bound, shouting that I'd called demons through the vents.

Funny thing—they didn't realize the vents *had been there first.*

The asylum welcomed me like a second baptism. White walls. Bleach. Whispering pipes.

The staff said the building used to be a hospital before the merger, but I recognized it from my dreams—the same corridors, the same pattern of vents as the ones above my pulpit.

The same hum under the floors.

Matron Hale came to me that first night.

She said nothing. Just stood at the foot of my bed, listening.

Then she nodded, as if taking attendance, and left.

The next day, a patient down the hall died in his sleep.

The walls hummed low and warm, like a satisfied throat.

That's when I knew.

The ledger had found its archive.

The church wasn't a building—it was a body. And this one still had blood left to move.

I began to preach again. Quietly, at first.

A few listeners—Boone, Nora Bell, one or two others.

We met after lights out, in Storage B.

The nurses thought we were trading cigarettes. We were trading forgiveness.

Every sermon began the same way:

I'd prick my finger, let one drop fall into a paper cup of water, and say the verse that never existed in the Bible:

"Three for the living, one for the lost,

hands open, hearts crossed."

Then I'd have each of them speak the name they wanted erased.

The ledger would hum. Sometimes the wall would knock—once for acknowledgment, twice for approval.

By dawn, one name from the patient census would disappear.

Balance maintained.

Boone called it witchcraft.

Nora called it mercy.

I called it administration.

It wasn't until the third month that the walls began to speak back.

You hear it at first like static, a hiss in the vents. Then it shapes syllables. Then words.

The voice is always polite, always maternal.

She called herself *Matron Hale.*

Said she kept the ledgers before I did. Said she still did.

I asked her how she survived the fire that supposedly killed her.

She laughed—softly, like water boiling.

"Fire burns the flesh," she said. "But names don't bleed easy."

From then on, she helped me choose.

She'd whisper which patients were overdue and which debts needed settling.

Sometimes she'd hum my psalm in the ductwork just to let me know she was awake.

They say I killed seven before they caught me.

That's wrong.

I balanced seven.

The eighth was the building itself.

Because one night the vents went silent. The hum stopped. The ledger went cold.

And I panicked. I thought God had gone deaf.

So I cut deeper. Hands, arms, throat—just to get its attention. Blood on the floor, words in the air. I begged for sound.

When it came, it came through the radio. Static first, then her voice.

"Cole," she said, "stop counting. I've already tallied the rest."

Then the light above me flickered, and I felt the warmth rise from the tiles, up through my knees, into my chest. The ledger turned its own pages without wind. When it stopped, my name had been added to the list.

That was the night I stopped preaching and started confessing.

Not because I was sorry. But because I'd realized I wasn't the prophet.

I was the punctuation.

Now the nurses call this place cursed. They're right.

They say the 13th floor doesn't exist. They're half right.

It exists where the walls have memory, and memory has appetite.

Every Halloween, when the veil thins and the clocks hesitate, she lets me preach one more sermon. You, Jack—*you're my congregation tonight.*

You keep your notebooks and your neat little rows of deaths and reasons. You think you're archiving confession, but you're archiving hunger. You're feeding it.

You've been taking attendance on the wrong floor.

Listen close—there's a pulse behind the pipes.

Hear it? That's her hymn.

She's already writing you in.

When the bell rings three times, don't look for the sound.

Look for the space between.

That's where she waits—the mother of ledgers, the Matron of Thirteen.

And if she calls your name, do what I did.

Answer.

Because silence is just another way of saying *Amen.*

CHAPTER 12
THE LEDGER OF THE DEAD

EPHRAIM COLE

When they shipped me here, I told myself I'd lay low, keep my head down. This place is a death sentence but I wasn't looking to die anytime soon.

Here's what I didn't know about this place. The walls in this building listen.

They listen, then swallow your secrets whole and spit them back out in voices only you know.

It took a few years, but I eventually found a laundry chute that leads to the thirteenth floor. Imagine that.

I laughed, like a kid who discovers a hidden cave. I think the powers that be forgot about the chute, I mean... they must have, or it would have been closed off, right?

Unless this place didn't want it closed, I've heard rumors, you know? Things happen in this place that shouldn't, that couldn't, and yet...

Anyway, I found the chute and then I heard a bell, low and clear, and I froze. Scared me shitless, it did. I for sure thought it was a ghost.

I've learned to respect the things that shouldn't be real.

The one who rings that bell? Not a ghost. That's Nora Bell. She appeared in the chute's mouth one day. "Teach me how to move the thread," she said. More of a demand, really.

I shrugged. "You already know how. You've been pulling it your whole life."

Her smile was dark, hungry. "No. I want the voice that comes after the bell. It spoke my name once, the way my grandmother did when she ran out of forgiveness."

How could I say no to that?

So we sat on that dusty floor, listening to the vents breathe. Sounds absurd, right?

Listening is the trade of both priests and predators. You know this.

The walls inhaled around us. Deep in the bowels of this place, a rusty relay clicked, and then, as soft as a whispered sin, a woman's voice drifted: "Stop."

"That her?" Nora gasped.

"I don't know," I admitted, and meant it.

Later, I threaded the red silk line through the ducts again and wedged a battered radio where the sample chute once lived.

I told myself I was holding up a mirror, but the building had its own design. From the thick silence, it spoke one name—Ephraim—tying command and absolution onto the same ribbon.

In that instant, I realized I wasn't the only one with a hand on the reel.

The bell rang again, pure and impossible.

Nora let out a laugh like a lock finally clicking open.

For a heartbeat, I saw a ledger float before my mind's eye—one column stamped DUE, the other PAID, a single red line binding them.

I still don't know what debt that is.

CHAPTER 13
THE MATRON HALE
ORIGIN FILE

JACK

The printer in Records wheezes like it's coughing up bones.

I've been feeding it requisitions all night—maintenance logs, staff rosters, anything with the word *Hale* still legible. The Warden said the fire files were sealed, but half the drawers down here don't even have locks, only dust. When the clock hit 3 A.M., the system spat out a folder that shouldn't exist: **HALE, M. – Personnel Archive / Ward C (1954–56)**.

I don't know if someone up-system pushed it or if the building decided I was finally ready to read its autobiography. Either way, I'm filing it before it disappears again.

(Recovered excerpts from North Wing Records — compiled by Nurse J. Steen)

Document 1: Internal Memorandum – St. Dymphna Hospital for the Incurable, 1954

FROM: Administrator W. Creighton
TO: Nursing Staff, North Wing
RE: Matron Appointment and Recordkeeping Initiative

Staff are reminded that *Matron Margaret Hale* has assumed full authority over Ward C following Matron Ellis's untimely resignation.

Mrs. Hale's proposed *Nightingale Ledger* program — a nightly census of patient vitals, behaviors, and "notable disturbances" — has been approved by Administration as a pilot study in institutional accountability.

Every nurse will submit a daily card tally to the Matron's desk before lights out. No exception.

Failure to report, or falsification of tallies, will result in removal from staff housing.

The Matron has the Board's complete confidence.

— *"Every number is a life, every life a record,"* she likes to say.

[Handwritten note, blue ink – margin, undated]
"Every number is a life."

First known usage of the ledger creed. That line still appears in the current policy manual—page 3, under *Data Integrity Statement.* Nobody remembers where it came from.

Document 2: Incident Report – Ward C Fire, 1956
Filed by: Nurse Ruth Canter (surviving staff)
Date: October 31, 1956
Time: 03:17 A.M.

I was completing medication rounds when I smelled smoke. The source appeared to originate from the linen chute near Room 13-C, though that room was sealed after the 1949 structural incident.

I called for Matron Hale via intercom. She did not respond. I proceeded toward the chute and noted excessive heat from the vent cover. I attempted to open the maintenance hatch but found it *locked from the inside.*

The corridor lights began flickering in sequence—one, two, pause, one, two, three. I remember it clearly because the pattern repeated like a heartbeat.

The smoke increased. I activated the fire alarm and began evacuating the patients, but the alarm failed to sound.

I then heard the Matron's voice over the ward speaker system: *"All accounts must reconcile in blood."*

The phrase repeated twice before static overtook the line.

I don't recall anything further until I woke in the east courtyard. The other nurses said I was found unconscious beside the bell tower, hands covered in ash.

Matron Hale was never recovered. Eight patients unaccounted for.

Structural engineers later reported "extensive heat damage localized to a non-existent floor."

End of report.

[Margin note – pencil, faint]

Fire contained itself. No scorch marks above or below.

13-C never existed on blueprints.

Ledger term appears *again.*

Document 3: Memorandum – Hospital Board Hearing Summary, 1957

Subject: Findings Regarding "The Hale Event."

Summary Prepared By: Chairman Harold Venn

Classification: INTERNAL – Level Red

Investigation yields insufficient evidence of foul play.

Matron Hale presumed deceased; body unrecovered.

Surviving staff report collective auditory hallucinations: whispering vents, rhythmic tapping, intermittent bell sounds.

The Board attributes these symptoms to trauma exposure and mass suggestion.

Remaining nurses transferred. Ward C officially decommissioned.

Note: During renovation, construction crew unearthed a metal filing cabinet fused to subfloor concrete. Contents: one partially burned ledger with handwritten entries in multiple inks and hands.

Last page legible entry reads:

"HALLOW-EVE, 03:00 — Account balanced. 8/8. Initiate dormancy."

The ledger has been placed in secure storage pending review.

DO NOT COPY.

[Margin note – typed addendum, 1974 reclassification form]

Ledger misplaced during facility merger; presumed destroyed in archive fire.

[Handwritten note – black pen, 2024, by J.S.]

Found it last week in a box labeled *"HVAC – Retired Parts."*

Still warm.

Document 4: Transcript Excerpt – Patient 312 ("Boone") Psychological Evaluation, 1957

Attending Physician: Dr. (name is blurred beyond recognition)

Patient: *Boone, Leonard*

Diagnosis: Schizoaffective, auditory hallucinations post-fire

Tape No.: 57-C-12

DOCTOR: What do you hear, Leonard?

BOONE: Bells.

DOCTOR: Bells where?

BOONE: Not where. *When.* They come when she calls roll.

DOCTOR: Who calls roll?

BOONE: The Matron. She says I'm late.

DOCTOR: Late for what?

BOONE: For counting. She says numbers get lonely when no one says their names.

DOCTOR: Do you know what she means by "numbers"?

BOONE: People. You. Me. Her.

DOCTOR: Does she ever say anything else?

BOONE: She says, "Tell Cole to stop writing in my book."

[Transcript ends abruptly – no closing statement]

[Margin note – red pen]

It is unknown who Cole is at this time.

Ledger = conduit.

Document 5: Building Plan Revision – 1961
Architectural Office Note (handwritten)

North Wing blueprints amended to remove redundant mezzanine reference between floors 12 and 14.

Structural engineer unable to verify any physical cavity but reports "anomalous acoustic chamber" responding to vibration frequencies at 440Hz.

Recommend sealing all service ducts pending inspection.

[Stamp: RESTRICTED – DO NOT DUPLICATE]

[Margin note]

That's A above middle C. The same tone the bells ring at now.

Coincidence my ass.

Document 6: Staff Memo – Facility Merger, 1999

FROM: Warden Charles V. Holt

TO: All Staff – Saint Dymphna

SUBJECT: Records Consolidation

All legacy files predating the 1978 consolidation are to be boxed and sent to Central Storage. No individual may retain originals.

Particular attention should be paid to the "Hale File," "Ledger Experiments," and "Fire Ward Reports."

Under no circumstances should staff attempt to recreate or continue any "ledger census" practices previously employed by Matron Hale or her successors.

If any documentation uses her handwriting, signature, or motto, it must be destroyed.

In the unlikely event of recurrence of "vent chatter" or "bell anomalies," contact Maintenance immediately. Do not record.

Administrative Reminder: There is no thirteenth floor.

[Margin note – faded marker]

Same warden. Same denial.

That memo's phrase—"vent chatter"—is the term Security uses today.

They think it's raccoons.

Document 7: Extract – Maintenance Log, 2007

Filed by: M. Gasper (Custodian, Night Shift)

Area: Sublevel B / Pneumatic Chute Access

Incident:

Technician reported light source behind sealed grate.

Upon inspection, saw what appeared to be an active service lamp suspended in midair beyond duct bend.

Audible breathing detected.

Technician refused to continue.

Supervisor notes temperature increase localized to his hand when he touched metal.

Action Taken: area resealed; report forwarded to Warden's office.

[Attached Note – from Warden Holt]

"Do not open what was meant to stay balanced."

[Margin note]

Holt retired 2008. Found dead in storage closet three weeks later. No sign of forced entry.

Door locked from *inside.*

. . .

Document 8: Personal Letter – Undated, unsigned, found in Matron's desk

My Dear Margaret,

They will not let me back into Ward C. They say the walls are unsafe, that the smoke weakened the beams. But you and I know the truth: the walls were never beams. They were ribs. And the vents were veins. And you only woke it.

I can still hear the bells. They sound like heartbeats slowed to prayer.

When you said, "Every number is a life," you forgot to mention: every *life* is a door.

And some of them open both ways.

Document 9: Audio Log Summary – Unlabeled Cassette (Recovered 2025)

00:12 – Static. Breathing.

00:24 – Woman's voice: "Matron Hale, evening census. Eight souls. Balance pending."

00:47 – Man's voice (Cole?): "You kept count all this time?"

00:50 – Woman: "Someone must."

01:06 – Male laughter, distorted.

01:09 – Woman: "Don't laugh, Pastor. I'm your proof of concept."

01:23 – Bell chime (three tones, descending).

01:25 – Tape warps. Male scream.

01:27–END – Reversal playback – whispering phrase: *"Ledger due."*

[Margin note – J.S.]

I found this tape in the same drawer as the extra radio.

I didn't press play twice.

Once was enough.

.   .   .

Document 10: Jack Steen – Personal Addendum (Undated, handwritten)

I spent the last hour transcribing the ledger's last page.

The handwriting shifts mid-sentence, from Hale's neat cursive to block print.

The final words:

"Account transferred. Steward: J.S."

I don't remember writing that.

I don't remember authorizing the entry.

But when I closed the book, the vents sighed—soft, like relief.

Maybe that's the point. Maybe someone always takes the ledger home.

Maybe the Matron doesn't haunt the building anymore.

Maybe she's waiting to clock in through me.

Document 11: Closing Annotation – System Metadata

FILE STATUS: Unresolved anomalies

USER: NURSE STEEN, J.

TIMESTAMP: 03:00 – October 31

ACTION: Save / Lock / Archive

(System alert: "Warning—file may be in use by another operator.")

Jack's Final Note (typed, unfiled)

The wall behind my desk just exhaled.

It smells like starch and candle wax.

I heard a pencil roll across the floor that I didn't drop.

And somewhere above me, a bell chimed once—no tone I recognize, but the rhythm felt deliberate.

Maybe that's how she says *goodnight*.

CHAPTER 14
THREADWORK

EPHRAIM COLE

Let me back up a little.

The first thing you learn in a locked place isn't humility or patience or the heavy dread of regret.

It's this: the need to move at least one invisible thing.

Maybe that's why, the first time my hands closed around the plastic reel of a dollar-store kite, I understood why men love control more fiercely than freedom.

Freedom is a word you write on a banner and wave at the horizon; control is the handle you keep hidden in your sleeve, thumb pressing down to feel the bite of the line.

Freedom is a theory. Control is a physics problem you can solve in your own lap.

When you get sent to a place like this one, you learn your first lesson right at the beginning at intake.

Intake is a lesson everyone here must learn. When you first come through, they strip you down, inventory your every possession, and smile like they've discovered a new species of disappointment.

Weapons vanish first—anything with an edge or heft. It's the rest that lingers, the ordinary crap that only reveals its danger after you've been here long enough to realize how very little you have: A plastic spoon, a shoelace, the elastic from a pair of boxers, all crowned with new names and darker purposes.

Intake is a crucible, and what survives the flames is not you, but a residue of your worst intentions.

One fall, they dumped a box of seasonal donations into the rec room. Halloween crap: tissue ghosts, off-brand candy, kites with cartoon pumpkins and tails the color of a warning label.

I still don't know if it was a mistake or planned on purpose. A test, maybe.

The COs cackled. "What, are they supposed to fly these in the yard?" They said it loud enough for us to hear, like the joke was the only thing we'd ever get for free. But I saw the way they lingered when the box landed. I saw the glint in their eyes, the hint of dread disguised as a dare. Because everyone knew the same truth: If you give a man enough string, he'll hang something.

Maybe that's what they wanted.

I snagged a reel, palmed it like it might explode, and popped off the cover with a thumbnail. The line was thin, translucent, wound so tight it could have garroted a sparrow. I learned its dialect real quick—the tiny shivers, the slack that told you it was snagged on something alive.

In my cell, I tied the line to a chewed-up chess piece, then to a thumb-sized eraser, then to a ball of dirty socks. Each time, I'd drop it in the hall and tug, watching the other men invent a logic for what they saw. A pawn scooting across tile is just wind, until it's not.

Men are born to make stories from nothing, doubly so when you put them in a box.

I started running lines in other places. I taped the filament low along the rec room benches, looped it around radiator fins in the library, ran it beneath the table so it would snap at just the right angle to trip up a bully's foot. You don't have to be subtle; you only have to be everywhere at once.

Men will believe in ghosts before they'll admit they missed a detail. Every tug of the reel was a dumb little miracle, a proof of concept: that the world could still be made to obey.

It wasn't about the pranks. Not really. It was about the pulse in my wrist when the line went taut, the whisper that no matter how deep the walls, I could still make something move. That's what hooked me.

I built my first kit from more than just string and trash. Two paper cups, a needle snatched from laundry—red thread, always red, because red is the only color that means anything behind glass.

I spooled it all together with the reel and practiced in the dead hours, when the world was silent and fluorescent shimmer. The trick was to smile through it, to look harmless, to make the right noises with the right faces so no one clocked the hunger under your skin.

A smile is a lockpick if you practice enough. Fools think violence is the only way a man can break open another man. It's not. Sometimes you need him to look away while you rearrange the room.

That was the groundwork. The show came later.

When they shipped me to another floor, the first thing I did was map the routes. You can't run a straight line in this building —the walls are hungry, the air thick with corners. It's not a space built for men, but for the memory of men. It wants knots. It wants friction.

I gave it those. I ran the line through vents and ductwork, always leaving slack, always leaving an escape. I knew the building was watching. I knew it liked a good story as much as the men did.

Nora Bell was the first to notice. She had the kind of smile you only see on scavenger birds—sharp, impatient, bright enough to make you flinch. She caught me reeling in a length of thread behind the nurse's station and grinned like she'd seen me with my hand in a real cookie jar.

"You're not scared of the red," she said, tilting her head. She always said it like an accusation, as if not being scared were the greatest sin.

I shrugged. "I'm scared of the day it stops answering," I told her, and it came out truer than I meant.

She reached for the reel, thumbed the handle, let the thread tremble under her finger. "You think it listens?"

"I think it listens when you want it bad enough."

She snorted, but didn't let go. "That's not science."

I let the silence stretch, watched her watching me, watched the way her hand hovered over the reel like it might bite.

That was the way with Nora. She lived in the cracks, in the places between rules. She'd been here longer than me—maybe longer than anyone. She knew every trick, every secret, every shortcut in the maze. I caught her slipping through locked doors twice, and both times she just looked at me and winked.

She watched me with her bird grin and said, "You're going to start a religion in here."

I laughed, maybe a little too loudly. "I'm just proving the walls aren't real."

She let the thread go, but not before giving it a sharp, deliberate tug. "Walls are real. It's what you build inside them that's fake."

She wasn't wrong. Neither was I.

That's the thing that keeps you pacing when the meds wear off: the idea that two things can be true at once, even if they cancel each other out. I think about it at night, when the lights flicker and the vents breathe and the only thing tighter than the thread in my hands is the memory of what I left outside.

The plan was simple.

I waited for Halloween, because even the most rational men go a little feral on the edge of a holiday.

The day before, I watched the orderlies string up orange

streamers and stuff the donation box with candy corn and wax lips. The nurses wore plastic bats on their lanyards. The guards paced the common room like lions in a cut-rate circus. The air crackled with expectation, and maybe fear, but mostly hunger for anything that wasn't more of the same.

Halloween is the only time a place like this admits it's haunted.

I set the circle at midnight, when the building got mean and the other men were either sleeping or pretending not to be. I used the red thread to mark the boundary, cups for the corners, and the reel for the heart. It wasn't a ritual, exactly, but it was close enough.

I pulled the line taut and waited.

The building answered with a shiver.

The vents thrummed. The cups rattled on the tile. Somewhere down the hall, a man began to scream—a low, animal sound, not meant for anyone but the darkness.

The men who were awake drifted to the common room, drawn by the sound or maybe by the promise that something had changed. They circled the line, careful not to touch, eyes wide.

I pulled the reel and made the cups jump. A few of them gasped. One laughed, high and desperate. I watched their faces flicker as belief warred with logic.

I was the force. But so was their shame. So was the architecture. I could feel the handle digging into my palm. I could feel the line running straight into the marrow of the place.

Nora drifted in last, hands jammed in her sweatshirt, eyes shining like she'd just seen a car crash and loved it.

She watched me without saying a word.

CHAPTER 15

THE BELL TOLLS BELOW

Every good show needs sound. In the cell, in the hull of a gymnasium, in the cut-off space between stacks of institutional bedding—if you want to move a crowd, you have to give them a frequency to rally around.

The first time I ever heard a bell ring in a place that didn't have bells, it didn't just surprise me. It rewrote me.

I remember the sound—thin, sharp, nothing like the bronze, slabby hush of church bells. This was the sound of two bits of scrap forced into a momentary marriage. The proof of collision: a tremor that said, 'something here refuses to stay quiet.'

There was this kid—a man, but young looking and small. What I liked about him was that he was forgettable.

I don't remember the shape of his face except in the way it looked when he was scared or when he was working a lock— either way, the same collapsing inward, like a star at the end of its contract.

The county system forgets them young. No matter what the murals say, nobody here expects a boy to come out whole. They send the best ones to the intake judge in chains, call them by last initials, assign a number, a bed, and a three-color schedule, and call that mercy.

The kid had a real name, but the floor called him Key, because he could let himself into anywhere the latch was tired. He was proud, at first. The proud that makes you easier to love and much easier to use. Where I come from, love and use aren't antonyms—they're just the two sides of the door.

I folded him into my kit. Taught him what needed teaching—how to see the thread, how to feel a tug through drywall, how to listen for the difference between a living bolt and a dead one. He was a fast study. Better than I'd been at his age, but then again, I never had anyone to teach me except the voices on the other side of the wall.

The rest of the pod kept their distance from us, which in context is a kind of respect. I made sure we always had something to trade. I put him on the grease line when I knew the COs would be distracted, and told him to watch how hands move when they lie. He watched. He learned. He copied the way I said "fuck" and "sure," and "maybe later" so that after a few months, people couldn't tell which of us was talking unless they looked straight on.

I didn't mind. It's easier to pass along a skill if you let it pass through you first.

There's an art to teaching a kid to be invisible. It's not just about quiet feet. It's about learning how to be the least interesting part of any room, how to let conversations slide over you like oil, how to stitch yourself to the perimeter so tightly no one can pull you free without tearing something.

I taught Key all of those things. He soaked them up. Sometimes it felt like I was pouring myself into a vessel with a hole at the bottom. But that's the job. You don't get to pick where your echoes end up.

The sound thing—that was his idea, originally. He wanted a way to mark time in the common room, saying it helped him keep the shift calendar straight. You learn the sun through the window, the shift changes by the stomping of boots, and the end of the day by how the hallway echoes after soup.

But this kid wanted precision. I think that's what drew me to him in the first place. I understood the need to nail each hour to a stake, to believe that every second lost was a crime against you personally.

There's a simple trick for this. Every room has a vent, and every vent has a shaft, and every shaft can carry sound if you clear the gunk and set up the right kind of line.

I showed him how to twist bedsheets into a tight, muscular cord, how to run it up through the vent cover without leaving a trace, how to tape a makeshift striker to the far end, and rig a counterweight with a sock full of ketchup packets or a sanded soap bar. I showed him how to find the resonance in a coil spring, how to tune it with dental floss and a bent paperclip, how to set the timing so that one tug equals one note, three tugs is a warning, and a steady pull is an alarm.

I want to say I did this for him, but the truth is I did it because I missed the sound of the ceremony. Not the prayer kind, but the kind that says, "We're all here. We're all listening." I guess that's close to religion, if you stand back from it. In the absence of God, you build your own rituals. That's the only way to survive the long blank stretches.

"What's the bell for?" he asked, the night we finished the prototype. It was a scavenged call unit from a dead bed rail, wired up to a length of dental tape and the metal guts of a pill bottle.

I wanted to tell him the whole story. How the sound of a bell can make men break ranks, can remind them they're still animals under all the starch and steel. How, in the old days, a single chime meant it was time to cover your tracks or say your last words or maybe look up, for once, and notice you were part of something bigger than your next meal.

Instead, I said, "Same thing a lighthouse is for. To tell people where they are when they're lost."

He looked at me, then at the makeshift bulb. "But this doesn't light."

"Light isn't the only way home," I said. I wanted to pat him on the shoulder or flick his ear, some normal affection, but that's a luxury in a place where every touch is a transaction. So I handed him the striker instead. He knew what it meant.

We made a proper bell later—found a length of soft copper under the rec room toilet, hammered it flat with the foot of a chair, bent it into an oval, and wired it so that a single pull would set it ringing for at least a minute before it wound down.

On a night with rain, when the noise of the world folds in on itself and everything echoes differently, I stationed him at the other end of the vent, the reel in his hand, the tricked-up clapper taped to a piece of broom handle.

"Three tugs, then strike," I told him. "Only once. Repeat it and you'll break the trick."

He did it. The sound was clean—pure enough to make men straighten, specific enough to be a message. I watched faces change. Fear and hope wear the same mask at first.

The COs looked at each other like someone had broken a rule they didn't know how to punish. The old men stopped playing cards mid-hand. Even the guys who hated us most admitted later it was a beautiful sound, or at least a novel one.

The bell worked too well. That was the problem.

With any good trick, the risk is always that it becomes more than a trick. The line between demonstration and ritual is thinner than any thread you can pull from a sheet.

I crossed it. We all did.

After a week, men started looking up when they cried, not out. They expected forgiveness to come down from the ceiling, not from the people they'd hurt. I suppose that's the true cruelty of visible miracles: they reassign responsibility. Nobody wants to be at fault when a ghost can do the job for them.

Key wanted payment. At first, I gave him stories about the other side of walls. The kind of talk boys use for armor. It wasn't enough. It never is.

He started snagging things off the staff. Not big stuff—just tokens, proof he could still get in and out of a place without being noticed. One day, he came to me with a real bell, small and cracked and old as dirt, the kind they keep in glass at the chapel for the priest to ring at funerals.

"Don't," I told him. "That kind of sound never leaves clean."

He just smiled and said, "You still need it, though."

He tried to ring it in the vent alone, one night, and dropped it. I heard it clanging in a place I couldn't reach, rolling down a duct the way a secret rolls down a hallway.

The next day, the COs did a sweep and turned his bunk into a crime scene. He got a week in seg and came out quieter than before, but I never heard him say "sorry." Not once.

Sometimes at night, I still hear the bell rolling. Down the duct, toward the dark. Like a name rolling down an empty hallway when no one claims it. I suppose that's what a legacy is, in here: the last sound you make when you've already left the room.

The boy with the bell taught me that wanting an answer is how you end up ringing a question until it cracks.

CHAPTER 16
ROOMS THE FIRE NEVER REACHED

I once kept a ledger, and I don't mean one of dollars or cents.

In the economy I'm describing, the sums never line up, mistakes are carved indelibly into the spine, and nothing can be crossed out.

The currency was human need, and the charge was regret that gnaws at your bones long after hope has fled.

Every time a man stumbled into my makeshift chapel—mouth raw with one hunger or another, craving oblivion, forgiveness, salvation, or the sweet release of death—I dipped my pen in black ink and wrote his name.

If he swore he'd glimpsed the light, or hallucinated the curve of a cross at the bottom of a Dixie cup, I noted the date in the margin. If he came back with proof—confession, compliance, or a new soul to step into his place—I'd award him a check mark, but always a crooked one.

Symmetry had no place in these transactions. Balance was a lie. This ledger was nothing more than a feeble act of stewardship, as if by naming every wandering sheep I could convince myself I wasn't the wolf.

I told myself I kept it to track the living. In truth, it was an inventory of the dying. There's a chasm between those two ideas —a chasm that, in the end, excommunicates you.

The night I dosed two of them—Looper, who apparently escaped once, far enough to cross the river and came back with the scars to prove it, and a man we called Dix.

Dosing them was supposed to be ceremonial, a pageant of mercy with the faintest flicker of hope. The temporary chapel was nothing but folding chairs under a single, buzzing fluorescent bulb, the air heavy with the scent of bleach and stale coffee.

In one corner, the chaplain strummed a hymn that had long since lost its tune, his fingers too arthritic to form real chords. The COs lounged by the riot-glass windows, studying their reflections like bored prisoners.

I measured the amber liquid in each Dixie cup with the cool detachment of a lab technician. But medicine, like faith, has its own caprices: sometimes it saves, sometimes it questions, and sometimes it's a slow pistol that takes its time squeezing the trigger.

Dix lifted his cup with vacant eyes and drained it in one smooth motion. Looper sipped his, winced, then met my gaze with a look that said, *You're not fooling anyone*—which, if I'm honest, was probably true.

The plan was to guide them through the night gently, to grant them dignity, maybe even something holy. But my calculations were off, or perhaps they never added up in the first place. Dix's breathing shallowed, quivered, then stilled altogether. A hush descended—a dense, expectant silence you only hear when a room full of people knows exactly what's transpiring and refuses to acknowledge it. For a moment, time paused. Then Looper blinked, coughed, and muttered "Shit," as though it was the only prayer left in him.

I wanted to believe I'd only pushed Dix to the threshold and that God had taken the final step. That comforting lie lasted until Tuesday morning, when Key showed up at the chapel door.

He looked like a map of mistakes—tattoos stretched over bad

decisions, grief pooling in his eyes like stagnant water. "He was scared," Key said. "He didn't want to go." Then he turned and walked away, leaving Dix's name echoing in my head longer than it ever had in my ledger.

The county did what counties do: they turned Dix's death into a file, stamped it with the wrong birthdate and a signature from a nurse who never even met him.

I did what I always did next: I tried to rewrite the story. I stared at the ledger for an hour, then drew a single line through Dix's name. But crossing it out didn't feel like erasure; it felt like folding a ghost in half. So I wrote the name again beneath the strike, hoping repetition might dilute the guilt. It didn't. If anything, each re–writing pressed down harder on my chest.

That was when I understood: keeping books for God is a losing game. He doesn't forgive arithmetic errors. He never tallies up the losses and calls it even. He lets the pages grow heavy with blood, sweat, and spilled hope until they're glued shut.

By the next Halloween, I vowed to do no one any harm. The ritual would be hushed, unobtrusive—no borrowed seconds at the bottom of a cup. The men still wanted the ceremony: chairs in a circle, two cups passed round, the bell that tolled their own mortality.

I obliged, promising them only fear enough to stay honest, then to send them back to their familiar nightmares—the way parents soothe a bad dream, teachers administer a test, preachers brandish Hell.

Nora sat watching, arms folded, exuding a contempt that felt colder than the chapel walls. When the others filed out, she drifted over to the ledger and tapped its cover, as if checking for a pulse. "What do you write," she asked quietly, "when the miracle fails?"

"I don't write anything," I lied.

"That's not how ledgers work."

I shrugged. "I'm changing the system." But I sounded like a man inventing new rules to lose another game.

When I moved into the not-floor—a place off the grid of normal time and consequence—I brought the ledger with me. It seemed fitting to bury the names in a haunt of warped reality, like tucking away the remnants of lost souls. The first night, I pried up a rotting floorboard and slid the heavy book beneath. The air shifted, as though someone had settled beside me on the cot, but I didn't look back. I listened for the distant chime of that bell and thought: Dix. Not a ghost, exactly—more like an impossible equation I'd never solve.

The next morning, Nora took the ledger from beneath the floorboards before I was awake enough to lie about it.

She placed it square in the center of the scarred table, between the remnants of our coffee and the cinders of last night's conversation.

She just sat there, arms crossed, gaze drilling holes through the battered cover, as if daring me to explain why I kept carrying it forward, year after year, like a priest refusing to retire his bell.

"You know they're not coming back," she said at last, voice steady but with a shiver at the edges, like a flag refusing to drop even when the wind dies. "The ones you lost. The ones you keep writing." She didn't look up, just traced her finger along the white scar at the bottom edge.

"I know," I said, because there was nothing else to say and everything else would be a lie. My own voice sounded unfamiliar, thin and brittle, the echo of someone who'd spent too long talking in empty rooms.

She shook her head, a fraction of a movement, but it landed like a verdict. "You write them in anyway. Even the ones who never stood a chance. Even the ones who slipped through your hands before you learned to spell their names." Her tone was soft, but the accusation was surgical. "Why do you do it?"

"That's the job," I managed, not sure if I meant it as defense or confession. "Somebody has to keep score."

Nora snorted, not in derision, but as if the answer were so monumentally inadequate it bordered on insult. "You really think anybody cares about your scorekeeping?" She pushed the ledger toward me, not gently. "You're not running a casino. You're not God's accountant. You're just a man with a bad habit and too much ink."

I stared at the ledger and thought about what it weighed.

Not the physical heft—though it was heavy, a hundred or so names, most of them only firsts or nicknames, two already blotted out with a line so thick it bled through three pages—but the way every entry landed on my chest and sat there, waiting for absolution that never came.

Maybe she was right. Perhaps the whole exercise was a fossilized superstition, a ritual too old to kill and too pointless to matter.

But there was a part of me, the feral part that still believed in omens and debts, that needed to feel the record mattered. That if I kept the list honest, the dead would stay where I put them, and the living would march in an orderly line toward whatever came next.

That if I could just account for every sin and every loss, I could pay off the balance and walk away clean.

Nora must have seen the calculation flicker across my face, because she smiled—a brief, knife-sharp flash of teeth—and said, "So who are you kidding, really? Me? Yourself? Or them?"

I thought about Dix's final moments, the way his eyes had gone glassy and fixed on a spot above my left shoulder, as if something important was waiting in the corner, just out of sight. I thought about Looper, still breathing, still waking in the dark with his hands around his own throat. I thought about every entry and every erasure, and about how every one of them was a little funeral I kept reliving because I had no idea what else to do.

"Nobody," I whispered, surprising myself with the honesty. "I think I just want to remember. Even the failures."

Nora's smile faded, replaced by something sad and surgical. "Then write that down," she said, tapping the cover. "Write the truth for once. You owe them that much."

I watched her for a long moment, knowing she wouldn't break eye contact, knowing she'd sit there until I either made my peace or let the page stay blank.

Finally, she laid her hand on the ledger, palm flat, and nudged it closer.

"Make it count," she said, "or stop pretending it does."

CHAPTER 17
SALT LINES AND PAPER CUPS

The stories here are fuel for the soul. And I'm not talking bedtime stories told when the lights are out.

I'm talking about the stories a place tells—what's baked into the bone, not the drywall. What you hear and what you don't, and what you choose to believe because, in places like this, belief is as good as oxygen.

That's how I first heard about Matron Hale.

Her legend stuck to every shift change like the congealed coffee at the bottom of the breakroom pot, bitter and perennial. The senior orderlies would drop her name as a threat, a promise, or a punchline, depending on the audience and hour.

"You want to be on time, kid," they'd say, "or Matron Hale will put you in the ledger."

"She doesn't do write-ups," the charge nurse barked once, "she does obituaries."

"Halloween's her birthday," whispered another, "and every year she claims a present."

You learn to listen from the edge of the conversation, chew the gristle, and spit out the parts you can't stomach. You add it to the private Bible you keep in your skull—the rules that matter, the deaths that count.

The first time I wore the vinegar tang of hospital air, I was just a guest. That was before. Before the chain, before the bus, before the windowless room with the steel table.

My mother had fallen, and from the way the nurses looked at me (never her), I was old enough to understand this was the first of her last times. I remember the building more than her. How it hunched against the sky, all gray stone and black glass, like a fossilized animal trying to rise. How it showed you every entryway but dared you to pick the right one.

The thing about this place, this asylum, is that it's a courthouse that lost its license. It wants you to believe it can judge. Sometimes it does.

In here, no matter if you're an inmate or an employee, we're all prisoners.

They strip you of everything with a cord or a clasp. Shoes become foam slabs. You get a jumpsuit in a color that means "safe to be in the hallway."

I took the county tour: holding cell, intake, sally port, then a corridor that stretched so long it folded back on itself, the lighting a punishment in its own right.

I arrived in the daylight, but it was always the same time inside—what my cellmate called "forever o'clock." The only difference was the noise: day and night had nothing to do with the sun but everything to do with the way the building vibrated with intention.

Every place has a pulse. But this one has arrhythmia.

The rhythm here was drum-tight, maintained by the guards who measured time in rounds and the nurses who measured it in pill cups. But all the real business happened in the off-beats—at the moments when the routine tripped or missed a step.

At 3 a.m., everything slowed, slowed so hard you could feel the air thickening with sleep and the possibility of mistake. It was the hour for ghosts and second thoughts. That's when I started noticing the edges of things.

The first thing I found was the chute.

It was supposed to be for laundry, but the sign said "DECON-TAMINATION ONLY," which meant it was everyone's secret. The camera outside its door had a red light, but it was dead—had been dead so long the tape over the lens was brittle with age. I watched the day orderlies toss bags through and never once saw them land. I asked one, once, "Where does it go?" and he said, "The incinerator," then smiled like a man who's never seen fire. The night I used it, I needed to be somewhere else. Not gone. Just changed.

It isn't a drop, not the way you think. Not a cartoon free-fall, not a screaming, flailing descent. It's a slide, a slow, cold conversation with metal and gravity.

You sit, you tip, you scoot yourself past the lip, and there's a moment where you're not moving at all—just suspended in the possibility of movement—before the air beneath you says now.

The chute isn't smooth or clean. The whole way down, it talks to your skin. It peels off the old you, cell by cell, and dumps you out into the dark, smelling like bleach and memory.

I landed in a subbasement that wasn't on any map. I know because I checked. I had memorized the fire evacuation sheets on every floor, the "IN CASE OF EMERGENCY" placards with their color-coded lines. This place wasn't on it.

It wasn't a room, exactly. It was a negative space, a corridor that ran parallel to nothing, lined in tiles that even the orderlies wouldn't bother to scrub. The air was stale, but the dust on the floor was new—like someone had swept, just for me. I followed the footprints until I reached a hatch I'd never seen before. Not a door. A hatch.

On the other side was the old maternity ward.

You know places like this from movies. The paint curled away from the walls in strips, like skin sloughing after a sunburn. The glass was frosted with years of condensation and sorrow, the beds lined up as if waiting for the next emergency. I wandered, because that's what you do: you look for the pattern, the story, the reason why the building let you in.

That's when I saw her.

She stood at the far end of the corridor, where the flicker from the emergency exit sign made the air look green. She wasn't tall or imposing. She didn't have the hunger of a monster or the fire of a saint. She had the posture of someone who'd waited here a long, long time and expected you to be on time, too.

"Matron Hale," I said, because sometimes the name is a password.

She didn't answer. She just smoothed the front of her uniform and walked away, expecting me to follow. So I did.

She led me to the old nurses' station, which was stacked high with binders and ledgers and the detritus of a hundred thousand forgotten lives. I rifled through them, hoping to find the one with my name. Instead, I found bracelets—plastic, cloudy, stamped with numbers and dates. All of them had an H at the end.

I thought of the stories: how the Matron kept a ledger, how she took Halloween personally, how she claimed a present every year. I traced my thumb over one bracelet and tried to imagine the wrist it had belonged to.

There was a ledger, too. Not one I wrote, not one for me. It was old, thick, heavy with careful ink. The handwriting was so neat it hurt to look at.

I paged through until I reached Halloween, 1987. At the bottom of the page, a name was added in a different hand—the script uneven, desperate, like a left-handed confession. There was no discharge date. Only a line, trailing off the edge of the paper, like a thought someone could not complete.

Matron Hale stood very close now. I could smell the starch from her uniform, the kind nurses ironed in when they wanted to feel invulnerable. She stared at the ledger, not at me.

"You waiting for someone?" I asked.

She didn't nod, but she didn't need to. The answer was already written. I put the book back where it belonged and closed the cover, careful not to pinch her fingers.

That's when I heard the bell.

You think a place like this would be full of bells, and you'd be right. Call buttons. IV pumps. The polite ping of the elevator when it arrives to collect a body.

But this bell was different. It was heavier, older, the kind of bell that rings for the beginning of something and the end of everything else. It came from behind the walls, vibrating the air rather than the ears. Matron Hale stiffened, her hands flattening on the counter.

It was time for her to go.

I watched her walk away, down the corridor where the lights had all burned out, her silhouette shrinking until she was smaller than my worst memory. I lingered, hoping she'd come back, but she didn't.

I still had the ledger's weight in my hands. I took it, because you always take the thing you're not supposed to. I hid it under a loose floorboard in the basement. If the hospital wanted to keep its secrets, it could work in its favor.

The next night, I came back.

The chute was colder, the ache in my skin deeper. The subbasement was darker, but the footprints were fresher. This time, there was someone else: a woman in scrubs, younger than Matron Hale, her hair pulled back so tight it looked like it might snap. She waited at the hatch with her arms crossed, her lips pressed flat with patience.

"You going to meet her?" she asked.

"If she wants," I said, because in places like this, you don't volunteer for anything.

"She'll want," the nurse said, and then she turned and led me up the corridor—away from the maternity ward and into a part of the building that didn't have a name.

It felt like hours, turning corners until I couldn't tell where we started. Until I couldn't tell if we'd started at all. There was no dust here, only echo, and the longer we walked the more it felt like someone else was setting our pace: someone with more time than either of us.

We passed a junction in the corridor and I glanced right, just for a second. Just long enough to see a bell on a wire. Just long enough to see it shiver.

The nurse kept moving, never looking back.

I followed, because that's what you do: you look for the pattern, the story, the reason why the building let you leave.

CHAPTER 18
NORA BELL'S MAP

Let's talk about Nora Bell.

Nora is the sound a lock makes before it clicks.

She's the sliver of dark between the edge of the door and the light beyond it, thin enough to slip behind a curtain rod and fast enough to vanish the second your eyes adjust.

Her face is a collection of sharp things: the hook of her jaw, the blade of her nose, the scary intelligence that gives the rest of us paper cuts just by looking.

If the world dealt out tools in a birth sack, Nora got a pair of pliers and a box of chalk.

She collects stories the way old men collect debts, and half the tales that drag themselves around the dayroom can be traced back to her mouth—told in a whisper or a dare or, sometimes, in a single raised eyebrow. Her eyes, fixed and unblinking, are the only things in the building that never flicker.

She found me before I found her. That's her style: get the jump, set the terms, make discovery seem like your own idea. I was at the end of an unremarkable breakfast when she dropped onto the bench across from me, her tray clattering like a starter's pistol. She didn't bother with hello.

"You're the man with the thread," she said, picking up a spoon and spinning it on its bowl. Her fingers traced invisible loops in the air, like she was already practicing sleight-of-hand with something too delicate to touch.

I looked past her, toward the glassed-in guard post, but she didn't flinch. The rest of the cafeteria was at war with its own boredom—plastic utensils snapped into shivs, toast crusts flicked like confetti, the louder men threatening to take hostages if the milk ever arrived soured.

Outside, the wind battered the window with a rhythm that sounded almost intentional.

"Teach me the reel," she said.

I set my fork down carefully, a courtesy to the space between us. "Why?"

She smiled, a flash of canine and calculation. "Because you're not the only one who hears the building breathe."

That's how it started: a recruitment, a negotiation, maybe a warning if you read it backward.

She knew about the thread. I'd spent the first two months here unspooling it like a conjurer, using the oldest tricks I remembered from the road—spilling salt, muttering over twine knots, convincing men who'd never feared death that a draft in the wall was something to pray against. Nora watched without blinking, collecting, storing, biding. When she finally spoke to me, I knew it wasn't just because she was curious.

She'd been living on the not-floor before I even knew it was more than a rumor. It's the floor no one wants to be on, where you're forgotten, discarded, vanished from memory.

Nora stole the old maps from Maintenance—one of the janitors owed her, though nobody knew why—and memorized them. She could tell you which vents connected to which rooms, which shafts ended in a dead drop, which ones carried the stink of bleach, or piss, or the smell of rain that always arrived a few minutes ahead of the storm.

She called it her "choir." If you pressed your ear against the right spot at night, she swore, you could hear voices carried through the ducts, humming their names in low, off-key chords. Some were the names of men who'd died here. Some were names that belonged to nobody.

"What names?" I asked her once, when we were alone in the solarium and the rain was at its loudest.

A flicker of mischief crossed her face, but she kept her eyes steady. "Ones you've tried to forget," she said, like she was already reading my obituary.

That was the hook, the challenge the old Nora would never have passed up.

I started meeting her in the library, the laundry, even the storage closet with its cracked blue tile and mop water that never dried. She'd bring a new artifact each time—a strip of gauze, a half-melted crayon, a feather plucked from somewhere unspeakable—and we'd test how each one carried sound.

The circle was her idea, a séance gone feral, using plastic cups instead of candlelight and thread instead of prayer. When we practiced, she was the only one who never pressed too hard, never forced the movement. She let the cups skate under her fingers, patient as a cat watching a bird remember how to fly. She had the stamina to wait for a draft. When the first ping came—a metallic twang, just a shudder in the cinderblock—she smiled and whispered, "She likes you." I wanted to ask who, but didn't.

Nora treated the whole building like a labyrinth engineered for her entertainment. She mapped out the guards' rotations, counted the seconds between each round, and even learned the way their boots changed tempo when somebody new was on shift.

She'd narrate her findings with a running commentary, delivered deadpan and rapid-fire as we jogged the hoops in the rec yard. "See that? That's Boudreaux. He's got a limp on the left and a wife who sends him meatloaf in Tupperware every Tuesday. The smell lingers till Thursday, easy." It was a joke, but also a weapon.

She cataloged everything, waiting for me to notice the pattern.

Late one night, Nora slipped into my cell and left a note under my pillow. The paper was torn from the back of a library Bible; the ink was a thumb-smear of mascara. It said, in her spidery hand: "Chapel. 4:17 AM. Don't be late or you'll miss the crescendo."

I lay awake for an hour, then two, counting the heartbeat pulse of the fluorescent lights and wondering what kind of crescendo a girl like Nora would have in mind.

At 4:15 I found her in the chapel, perched on a pew like a crow. She'd already yanked the speaker cover off the wall and fed a length of dental floss through the vent grille. "Sit," she said, not looking up. I sat. She wrapped the end of the floss around a cheap ceramic angel, wound it tight, and waited.

"You know what confessions sound like in this place?" she asked, voice almost reverent.

I shrugged. "Like insurance."

She grinned. "Wrong. They sound like ice melting. Nobody means a word of it, but the drip never stops."

I watched her tighten the line, stretching the floss until it thrummed with tension. The vents started to hum. At first, it was just a low, static rumble, the kind of white noise you can tune out if you try. But then a pattern emerged, like a hidden message in the hiss.

Nora's eyes went wide. She turned to me, her face lit by the exit sign's red glow.

"Matron," she whispered, and the voice in the vent said her name back to her, slow and deliberate: "Nora." It sounded almost human, but not quite.

That was the first time I believed her, not in ghosts, exactly, but in the power of obsession to carve its own reality. The voice knew her. It might have known me, too, if I listened hard enough.

We spent the next week experimenting.

Nora pilfered a stethoscope from the infirmary and used it to chart the sound tunnels inside the walls. We found spots where the voices were louder—especially near the old laundry chute, where the stone went soft and damp. Sometimes we'd hear more than one voice: a chorus, a bickering, a rapid shuffle of desperate words like the world's worst party line.

We took turns guessing who the voices belonged to. Nora got good at impressions, mimicking the warden's drawl, the night nurse's gurgle, the men on lithium's flat affect. But the one that made her shiver was always the same: Matron Hale, the lost queen of the not-floor.

"She knows things," Nora said, cradling the stethoscope like it was an infant. "Things about you. About me."

I tried to laugh, but the joke stuck in my throat. "She's got a radio. Maybe half a radio. It's feedback. An echo chamber."

Nora looked at me, all irony gone. "You don't get it. It's not the radio. It's the building."

There's a moment in every con where the mark wants to believe. You see it in their eyes: the hunger, the helplessness, the trembling need to surrender to something bigger than themselves. I'd made a career out of that moment.

But sitting next to Nora in the dark, listening to the walls declare her name in a voice that wasn't quite possible, I felt something like pity for myself.

I started seeing Nora more often in the periphery after that. Sometimes she'd vanish for days, then reappear with new maps, new scars, new stories. She recruited two more girls—one with a knack for picking locks, another who could sleep through the apocalypse and wake up smiling—and together they built a cartography of the unseen.

I became the only male allowed in their sessions, the token cynic, a role I played with increasing discomfort.

One afternoon, while we were tracing a new threat line through the admin wing, Nora paused, pressed her ear against the air vent, and motioned me over to listen.

"Him," she said, pointing at me. "It's him."

I knelt and caught the end of what she'd heard: my name, whispered in a breathless, gulping panic, as if whoever was saying it was running out of both time and air.

I pulled back, stunned, and for a moment, Nora looked almost sad for me.

The next morning, I woke up shivering. Somebody had cut the heat again. The radiators were forever on the fritz, but this time the cold felt personal, like the building was returning my disbelief with a grudge. I could see my breath, taste rust when I swallowed. The walls creaked and sighed, brittle as old bones. I wrapped myself in both blankets and tried to think, my mind drifting to the girl who'd slept in this cell before me.

Her name was Marie. She held the record for the longest streak in solitary, four months without a single visitor, before they finally found her hanging from an exposed pipe. Her death hadn't surprised anyone—the guards said she'd been hearing things, talking to herself—but it was still a paperwork nightmare.

They'd shuffled the rest of us around while they scrubbed her ghost off the ceiling.

I ended up here. My consolation prize. My haunted inheritance.

At breakfast, I asked Nora if she'd heard a girl like Marie on her stethoscope. She gave me a long, curious look but didn't answer.

"What did you hear?" she asked instead. "Your name, or hers?"

Both, I almost said. Maybe neither. But Nora was already up and moving, gathering her girls, plotting new routes. She was more frenetic than usual, a wind-up toy spinning toward some inevitable, destructive release.

I followed her around the yard, into the service corridors, past the infirmary and the boiler room and the chapel where the voices first found us. We ran thread line after thread line, a tangled web of floss, lies, and loyalty. By evening, the layout was complete. I could see what she'd done and where it was going: everything pointed back to the same, inevitable spot.

The not-floor.

The place where her ghost lived. The place where she said

she'd hear the voices, even if she ended up dead. I thought about warning her, but knew it was useless. We were way past the point of reasonable doubt. So I let her go.

4:17 came and went. I spent the night in my cell, half-expecting her to slip another note under my pillow, half-expecting to wake up with the cold, dead weight of her expectation on my chest.

I didn't expect the sirens or the lockdown that followed. The guards hit us with clubs and shouted over the alarms: "No talking! No moving! No goddamn whispering!" Nobody listened.

The whole cellblock erupted with the panic of a thousand unanswered questions, one name rising above the rest: "Nora! Nora! Nora!"

It was the chorus we'd been waiting for, all static and terror and heat. I sat on my bunk and watched the chaos spin itself down to a miserable, exhausted hum. I knew how long that kind of silence could last. Weeks, if you kept your nerve. Months, if you were running a long con.

I lay back, closed my eyes, and thought of her perched on a low beam in the not-floor, grinning like a banshee when they found her. They'd say it was a suicide, a miscalculation, a filthy prank gone wrong.

I'd say she played us all, including the ghost of a girl named Marie.

CHAPTER 19
MAINTENANCE MANUAL ADDENDUM – ACOUSTIC PROTOCOL

(Revision 3 – Facilities Engineering Reference Document, 1989)
   (Recovered from Sublevel Archives, Section 3-B, by Nurse J. Steen)

Section 1: Purpose

This addendum provides updated operational guidance for staff encountering **Acoustic Recurrence Phenomena (ARP)** within ventilation systems, drainage conduits, or other hollow infrastructural components of the North Wing.

ARP presents as sustained rhythmic resonance ("bell tones," "duct murmurs," "heartbeat tapping") not linked to mechanical malfunction or human speech.

While previous facility reports classified such events as *"ventilation echo anomalies,"* updated documentation recognizes ARP as an *environmental persistence artifact* tied to pre-merger architecture.

Section 2: Detection

1. **Do not pursue sound origin.**

2. If source appears to move through ductwork, note the pattern but refrain from physically following.
3. Should frequency register between 438–442Hz (A4 tone), record duration.
4. Under no circumstances respond verbally to the recurrence.
5. If tapping includes three pulses followed by one pause, evacuate the immediate area.

(See Appendix A: Known Rhythmic Sequences — "Census Pattern.")

Section 3: Containment Procedures

- Temporarily seal vents using polymer compound 4B. Do not weld, as heat encourages reactivation.
- Disconnect local intercom systems to prevent cross-channel interference.
- Log event time under "Environmental Disturbance – Class C."
- If "voice replication" occurs (staff name spoken through duct), respond with silence.
- **Never acknowledge roll call.**

Section 4: Historical Reference

Recurrence of ARP events aligns with anniversary dates of **The Hale Event (10/31)** and **The Cole Dismissal (07/12)**.

Acoustic mapping indicates tonal activity concentrated around sealed access labeled "M-Floor."

Engineering Note: "M-Floor" corresponds to no physical location on current schematics. Likely vestige from obsolete record numbering (see *Deleted Floor 13* memorandum).

. . .

Section 5: Personnel Guidance

Persistent exposure to ARP may induce:

- Elevated heart rate in sync with resonance
- Perception of whispering or roll call through ductwork
- Compulsion to document or respond to pattern

Staff demonstrating these symptoms should report to infirmary and surrender written notes for archival.

All such notes become the property of the Warden's Office.

Someone added my name decades before I was hired.

The sound file reference number for ARP-J1 links to a reel-to-reel tape. It plays my voice, asking if anyone's still on shift.

If I ever doubted this place is haunted, I don't anymore.

Final Page Annotation (Typed, Unsent Memo)

TO: Warden Holt

FROM: Lead Engineer B. Carrow

SUBJECT: RE: 13th Floor Duct Network

During inspection we found junction box stamped *M13*.

It shouldn't exist.

It vibrates on its own—slow, even rhythm.

Recommend we leave it sealed.

Recommend you stop saying her name over the intercom.

CHAPTER 20
RED THREAD, WHITE KNUCKLES

EPHRAIM COLE

A trick isn't a trick until you can repeat it under harsher conditions, with a meaner audience.

Tonight, as the fall wind turned the city sharp and sour, was my first real test. This wasn't a parlor or a dorm or some bored therapist's office. The puckered, jaundiced halls of the asylum didn't make for great acoustics, but they had the kind of crowd you can't bluff: men who'd already lost everything, who'd stabbed, shot, and starved their way through life and had nothing left but their own minds and the slow acid of memory.

If my trick failed, it would fail spectacularly—my first and last gig among the lifers and the doomed.

Three nights ago, I slipped down to the sublevel with a length of red thread spooled beneath my tongue. I thumbed it flat against the roof of my mouth, sneaking past the septic gurneys and mop buckets that doubled as the janitorial graveyard.

Nora, who had a better sense of timing than God, met me at the bleeder's corner and didn't even blink when I pulled the slimy red mess out of my mouth. She just grinned, teeth like chipped dice, and held out her palm.

We spent the next two nights rigging the ducts. The thread

was a guide-wire, running from my bunk up through the vent, across the service pipes, and into the old admin annex where the condemned men took their last meals. We laid the line, tucked it into the gaps, pinned it with chewed gum, and every so often Nora would whistle low and say, "You know, they'll just kill you for this." I always shrugged. "At least it won't be boring."

The next step was the radio, a prehistoric walkie that probably saw action in three wars and at least one exorcism. I'd bribed the night nurse with a promise to curse her ex-husband's next marriage, and she handed it over without even asking for collateral. I wedged the transmitter at the pneumatic hatch, batteries fresh, mic hot, and set the squawk to max gain. If it worked, I could pick up every echo from the test chamber. If it failed, maybe I'd go deaf before the guards punched my lights out. Nora didn't ask what frequency I'd picked. Instead, she watched me slap the duct tape around the mouthpiece and said, "You're making an altar."

"Not an altar," I corrected. "A mirror."

She scanned the work, her eyes narrowed and flickering, like she was watching every move for weakness. "Mirrors still show you something," she said. "Even if you don't want to see it."

I wanted to say something clever, but in that moment, I realized she didn't mean the radio, or the vent, or the trick at all. She meant me.

The supplies were the hard part. Real salt was contraband, but the kitchen let me handle the snack inventory, so I ground up pretzel rods in a plastic bag and called it kosher. The paper cups came from the laundry, scored and bent into makeshift bells. We painted them with the ink from old library books, melted the covers down to get the right char, and strung them along the thread until the line sang with every draft.

Then we waited. Two nights, then three, then four, until the guards got bored and the new arrivals stopped screaming through the walls. It's important to blend in, even when you're planning a spectacle.

The night of the trick, the men gathered in the rec room like a murder of crows. Hjalmar, the tattooed anarchist with hands bigger than my head, brought his chessboard and set up shop near the vent. Raheem, the polite bank robber who never swore and treated every sentence like a contract, offered to deal black-jack to pass the time. A few stragglers from the psych wing shuffled in, their paper slippers stained yellow, eyes darting from the TV to the moonlit bars.

No one spoke above a whisper. No one sat with their back to the door.

I knelt in the center, the reel of thread running from my palm up through the duct, and tried not to think about how easy it would be to garrote myself if I botched the timing. Nora stood just outside the circle, a lookout but also a witness, arms folded tight, jaw set. She looked like she wanted to kill me and also like she'd kill anyone who touched me. That's love, in its way.

I gave the signal—two quick coughs, then a click of the tongue. Nora waited, lips barely parted, and then tugged the thread. The bells skated down the line, brushing the vent's ribs and making a sound like wind chimes at the bottom of the sea. Every man in the room stiffened, their eyes drawn upward to the silver-gray line, listening for the code in the clatter.

For a second, it was just noise, the idle trembling of a hack con. But then the radio spat static —a white-hot hiss —and the hatch hissed open on its own. That was expected—solenoid release, nothing special. But the sound that came out of the vent wasn't the expected echo.

It was a ping, a perfect sine wave, higher and cleaner than any frequency I'd dialed. It was a voice, but not in any language I spoke; more like the memory of a voice, played backward. The bulb on the dead call unit—supposed to be cut off from the grid—glowed once, a single red pulse.

"Did you—" Nora started.

"No," I said, and for a heartbeat, the room was mine again because my fear outran hers.

The men stopped shuffling, stopped breathing. Even the guards in the corridor must have felt it, because the usual threats and catcalls died mid-word. We all drowned in the silence before the next noise.

We tried again. This time, the thread vibrated so hard it burned my fingers, and the cups snapped together at the midpoint, fused by static. The first ping returned, then a second, higher, in perfect counterpoint, like two bells in a duet, each cutting through the marrow.

The radio was off now—dead as stone—but the duet kept going, louder, until the ductwork hummed like a tuning fork and the call unit stuttered and flickered with wild red Morse.

That's not how physics works. That's not how any of this works.

The men recoiled, muttering half-prayers and half-threats. Hjalmar tried to stand but his knees buckled. Raheem slid the deck off the table, cards flapping to the dirt like grounded birds. The chess pieces rattled and fell, the pawns lined up like tiny soldiers waiting for a command that would never come.

No one wanted to ask if it was real. No one wanted to ask what it meant.

I stared at Nora, but she didn't look back. She stared at the hatch, her eyes wide, her mouth open, like she'd just seen herself through a two-way mirror and didn't like the reflection.

That's when I decided to confess. If the building was going to take my trick, it could have my story too. Stories are lighter than ledgers. Sometimes they even float.

I made my move.

CHAPTER 21
THE HATCH THAT BREATHES

You can prepare for every contingency, spin up a whole doctrine on risk, and still, the only thing that will truly fuck you is the one contingency that sounds like your own voice shouting from the vent at three a.m. with no one else awake to witness it.

I had considered every scenario for this night's experiment. Questioning. Catastrophe. Nora hurling a shoe at my face. The men snapping and pulling me limb from limb out of boredom or bloodlust. I'd even diagrammed on the back of a legal pad how quickly I could unscrew the phonograph's horn and use it as a weapon if the mood shifted from séance to shiv.

I'd refused to predict what would happen if the magic actually worked.

But nothing in my battered catalog of practical theology, nor in my memory palace of grifts and callouts, had prepared me for the first word out of that iron vent.

Not "Pastor." Not "Cole."

Ephraim.

In a voice as familiar as the old hymns, as inescapable as the stink of disinfectant in the mess hall, as direct as the sight line a judge uses to pin your humanity to the wall before stripping it away.

Ephraim.

Hissed as a summons—not a title or a threat, but a call to come inside before the dark closed in. A sound that reanimated my childhood in an instant, and made my entire chest vibrate with shame and longing and a pothole sense of dread.

The men in the circle looked at me—not at me, but through me, as if the name had knocked a temporary window in my skull and what they saw on the other side was a boy in a suit two sizes too big, a plastic cross sewn to his collar, walking the midnight aisle of First Bethel looking for a mother who was always already gone.

I could feel each of their hungers reaching out, tentative and electric, like fingers testing broken teeth.

The next word wasn't any easier. It was a name I hadn't uttered in this place, not even in the privacy of my own cell, where nothing is ever private, not even your nightmares.

It belonged to a woman who taught me scripture in the brutal way only a person who's been abandoned by God can teach it: over kettle burns and cryptic hexameter, by candlelight and switch.

She'd vanished from church before my voice cracked. She haunted my first theft, the ledger I'd rewritten with a trembling hand and then hidden under a loose board in the creche.

The name was the password to a secret I'd meant to bury, now exhumed by a mouth that couldn't possibly know it.

Not Nora, not the Warden, not the nurse with the silent clipboard and the serial killer's patience—they couldn't have set this up.

I tried to calculate the odds of a random voice from the vent landing on that exact name and I came up with zero, then subtracted a thousand from that.

The bulb above the circle snapped into an ugly strobe, spewing blue-white light at migraine tempo, the way an old projector flickers out the last seconds of a reel.

Every face in the cellblock washed over into bone and crater, eye sockets crawling with shadow. The table at the center, the so-called altar, glared pale and skeletal. Even the phonograph in my hand, that precious decoy, seemed to twitch against my palm, writhing like a garter snake on a cattle prod, or a tongue under anesthesia, or some other small, persistent animal convinced it could buck off the inevitable.

Nobody was looking at me now. Not really.

The men—the brutes, the lifers, the scattered collection of believe-what-you-want-and-fuck-you-for-trying   types—were transfixed by the vent, the table, the slow-motion suicide of the cigarette burning down into Pastor Thiel's webbed and callused thumb.

There's a moment in every con where the audience stops seeing you and starts seeing what you want them to see, and this was that moment, stretched out over a vise of hunger. Hunger for spectacle, for absolution, for the ghost of a chance they'd been wrong about everything.

Hunger is the engine of belief, and these men were running on fumes.

My mouth catapulted ahead of my mind, as it always does in these situations—any situation with enough metaphysics to choke a theologian.

"Matron Hale," I said, not raising my voice, because the trick to commanding a room is the same as commanding a dog: you whisper, and make the world bend in to hear you. "We're listening."

For half a heartbeat, the only answer was the sound of skin sizzling under ash. Then the vent replied, a static-rippled stutter like the oldest PA system in the universe, caked in decades of grit and sorrow.

"Ledger's due," it breathed. "Two souls and yours." I felt the syllables slice right through the chalked circle, through the hem of my shirt, into the old scar at my navel.

Nora, who'd been dead silent up to this point, started shaking.

Her hands bunched in her lap, fingers curling in on themselves like spider legs trying to crawl back into their own thorax.

"She's real," she said, and I could not tell if she was about to projectile-vomit or pray, or if she even knew there was a difference anymore. Her voice was so thin that it barely survived the trip from her lips to the meat of my ear.

I wanted—violently, obscenely wanted—to believe the radio was just glitching, hocking up residual tape, some leftover from a decades-old fire drill or a janitor dry-mocking the system. Maybe a busted loop of someone calling for a lost cat, or a therapist warning about the dangers of isolation for the institutionalized.

But the batteries weren't just dead; I'd exhumed them myself and lined the copper contacts with nail polish, for insurance. The radio was a corpse. The call system had been gutted for scrap before my last stint upstate. All that was left of the duct was a rusty esophagus, and tonight it was possessed by something that spoke my name in the first language I ever learned: threat.

The memory snapped back, too fast, too hot.

The ledger. The ledger I'd forged, the one with numbers rearranged like a child's ransom note.

I saw myself sweating over the pages, ink bleeding through to the board underneath, hands shaking so bad I almost signed the wrong name.

I remembered the loose floorboard, the hollow thunk of hiding it, and the moment it clicked shut—a sound that meant "safe" the way a gun hammer means "final."

Then, as if my skull had become the world's shittiest theater, I re-lived the twilight hospital corridor, the last time I'd seen my mother, her wrist banded in hospital plastic, the same white with blue letters as the ones they zip-tie on us now.

H, in permanent marker, the first initial of the only woman who ever taught me how to be cruel.

The nurse with the dark thermos, the one who always looked at my hands instead of my face, the one who said nothing but always watched. I wondered, with a desperate scientist's detachment, if the wire in his pocket would pick up a ghost's voice, or if it would just record the arrhythmic chorus of our collective heart rates, spiking and dipping like the EKG of a very bad night.

There was another sound, under the static—a noise I'd been trained since altar boy days to recognize as sacred. The chapel bell, a steel bastard that hadn't rung since the riot, began tolling in the background, each note so faint you had to listen through your teeth just to catch it.

Once. Twice. Three times.

Except it wasn't ringing; I realized with a growing, dental horror that the sound was actually coming from inside the vent. Something was tumbling down the ductwork, pinging the bolted seams at regular intervals, working its way past dust and rat bones, perfectly matching the tempo a priest uses to swing a censer at a child's funeral.

Every pass through the circle made the men flinch, as if at any moment it would drop out and land in the middle of our so-called altar, proof positive that hell had a mailroom and we were on the delivery list.

Nora started to smile now, wide and wet, the way a person does when they've finally caught the scent of the thing that's been hunting them their whole life. It was the happiest I'd ever seen her, and that was the most terrifying part.

I closed my eyes, just for a heartbeat, hoping the other senses would shut up and let me think. In that pitch-black second, I was nobody's pastor, nobody's con man, nobody's prisoner of record. I was a child again, under a leaking sheet-metal roof, listening for the Morse code of God in the rain on a coffee can.

Each drop was a message: Hide. Wait. Listen. Survive.

When I opened my eyes, the nurse was already moving. He stepped lightly over the chalk circle on the floor, as if it might burn him. His face was glassy with sweat and his cuffs were rolled so high you could see the blue map of his veins.

He reached for the thread I'd strung across the altar—a thread meant for show, for theater, for giving the crowd a proof they could see and touch.

He didn't hesitate. He pinched it between thumb and forefinger, and every man in the room inhaled as one.

You can make a miracle.

You can fake a miracle.

You can never control the moment someone else decides which it was.

CHAPTER 22
MATRON HALE'S HOUR

Let's talk about the ledger.

The one under the floorboard isn't mine, and that's the worst part. My ledgers are smoke and whispers, written in codes only I remember, each line a debt or a favor I'll one day collect.

This book, though, is older. Heavier. Leather binding so ancient it flakes at touch, catacomb black. The pages inside are yellowed, almost brittle, lined with a pitiless precision. The ink— its odor is sour, cloying, like the ghosts of dead solvents.

Smells like a different decade, or a time when men believed the pen could still outpace the knife.

The hand that wrote these entries was steadier than mine tighter, as if each loop and crossbar were a stitch in some private wound.

It spelled out everything: patient ID, date of intake, date of release, even cause of discharge, in a clerk's slanted hand—a surgeon's, maybe.

Some of the names I know, most I don't. But every page is haunted by the same date, marching through the years. Halloween. Listed in blank, in red, in double-underlines, like a drumbeat nobody else could hear.

Some of the guys upstairs call it Devil's Night. The rest don't call it anything at all.

The pattern is clear if you want to see it.

Every Halloween, there's an entry that shivers the paper: someone checked out, or checked in, or checked out sideways—sometimes discharged, sometimes "discontinued" in a block of bureaucratic blue.

One year—1987—the entries stop cold. No more lines, just a white expanse where the future should have been. At the bottom, in a different hand and different ink, there's one final name.

I won't write it here. A name like a curse, tucked under a date that's two weeks after Halloween.

No signature. Just a long dash running under the line, tapering into nothing, like the writer meant to come back and finish it but couldn't.

I want to think I cracked the pattern, but really it's more like a stain that seeps into anything left too close, too long.

The ledger is a cheat sheet for the building, a history written by the unburied. No one ever asks who kept it, or why, and nobody does the math on how many hands it passed through. I'm not sure when it ended up under my floorboard, but once it did, it was mine.

Even if I never wanted it.

For years I've told men they could be born again if they stepped to the edge. It's my best con—if you believe in it, it works. If you don't, you still get to watch someone else try.

I lifted the line from Dr. Hale, who ran "procedural interventions" back before the board shut her down. Controlled pain, breathwork, obedience as a kind of exorcism. She called it "Threshold Practice," which sounded like yoga for war criminals.

I hated her for it, but I used it anyway.

The first time I saw her ledger, I felt like a dumb child discovering a magic trick after the party's over. The same symbols, the same shuffles, only her big finish was a vanished girl and a concrete slab for a tombstone.

I should have burned the book the second I found it.

Instead, I just closed it, slid it back into its hiding place, and told myself I was preserving evidence for the day somebody finally cared as if that would absolve me.

I tell all this to the vent tonight. "She taught me how to do it," I whisper. "If you're still here, you already know that."

The vent runs above the north wall, right where the ledger lives. Sometimes, when I'm too deep into the pages, I hear a scuffle through the duct—a cough, a shoe scrape, a sigh bloated with boredom. It could be a rat, it could be a detail, but every time it happens, I see her name at the bottom of the ledger, and I lose a day or two to the walls.

The building answers me, always. Tonight it's just the slow inhale of settling plaster, the bass thud of some pipe kicking awake for the heat. Not words, but the tone of someone closing a book and putting it back on the shelf. Like a reminder that every ledger has a reckoning, and mine is due.

A click echoes in the hall. Fluorescent grid flickers alive, humming with that insect-light that makes even new concrete look sick. I hear the warden's step before he turns the corner— hard soles, no hurry. He waits at my door, doesn't bother with a knock, just stands there until I open it. When he smiles, it's a performance for the cameras, not for me.

"Up," he says.

He's not alone. Two guards stand behind him.

I look at my hands—still stained with old ink, knuckles gone white from clenching the ledger. It doesn't matter that the book is hidden, or that I'd shored up every lie I'd ever needed.

The warden's smile is a summons, and I know from long practice that when the system calls, it's best to answer before it asks twice.

"Now?" My voice is paper-dry.

He squeezes the bridge of his nose. "I didn't come down to wait."

I almost laugh, but my jaws too tight. "Right," I say, and drag myself out of my cell, past the ledger's hiding place, trying not to think about the signature line at the bottom.

The hallway's colder than it should be for October, and the lights strobe as we walk. I keep my head down. The warden walks ahead of me, a shadow with a face; the two guards walk behind me.

The building watches us as we go, listening. I can hear it, like the hush before a verdict.

We reach a room and the warden gestures for me to go inside. Two chairs, a desk, and a window that doesn't open. He closes the door behind us and sits, lacing his hands in a way that says this is a confession booth more than an office.

"You're probably wondering why you're here," he says.

He slides a folder across the desk, creased and stamped with the word DELTA in red. I don't touch it. He waits, watching my reaction like a scientist with a scalpel.

"You'll be running a new group," he says. "Starting tomorrow."

Fuck. Warden does these things when he doesn't want to spend money hiring more staff. It never ends well.

His tone makes it clear: this isn't a reward. It's a test. Prisoners get promoted when the system wants to see how much they'll endure before breaking.

"What's the catch?" I ask, my voice softer than I mean it to be.

He shrugs, but his eyes are hungry. "The state's watching. You run a clean group, nobody gets hurt, and the pilot goes public. You make a mess, you go back to the hole. Maybe farther."

I want to argue that I'm not the reason the old programs failed. That the ledger under my floor is just a fossil, not a prophecy. But the words clog in my throat. Hale's name floats up from the paper, unfinished.

"Understood," I manage. "Who's my intake?"

He smiles again, with too many teeth. "All new faces. Some tough cases. They want to see if your method really works, or if it's just stories."

He stands, gathering the folder, and I know the meeting's over. "Be ready, twelve-hundred sharp. Bring your A game."

I nod, hoping he'll leave. Instead, he lingers at the door, looking softening just a little.

"For what it's worth, you're the only one who ever made them listen." He taps his temple, a gesture of respect or warning. "Don't waste it."

The door clicks shut, leaving me with the hum of the lights and the sour taste of old ink. I sink into the chair, stare at the folder, imagine the ledger under the floorboard swelling with another decade's worth of names.

When the shift change sounds through the pipes, I get up, change into the old blues, and start rehearsing my lines for tomorrow. The building is quieter now, like it's waiting to see what I'll do next.

I have a dream that night, or something like it. In the dream, the ledger is open on my lap, but the pages are blank except for one column. Not names, not dates. Just a tally mark, over and over, until the ink seeps through and stains my hands.

The morning comes cold and quick. I line up outside the group room, feeling the weight of the building on my back. The new intakes file in one by one, and I recognize none of their faces. They sit, restless, waiting for the show.

I start with the oldest trick I know: "Welcome to Threshold, gentlemen." I gave this place a name because names hold meaning. My voice has never sounded less convincing.

They stare back, hollow-eyed, but a few of them lean forward. I tell them about rebirth, about transformation. I tell them every story I've ever stolen. None of it feels real.

I think about the ledge under the board, the unfinished line at the bottom. I wonder if I'll ever get to write my own name there, or if someone else will do it for me.

The group is silent, but they're listening. The way the building listens, the way the vent does. Waiting to see which one of us breaks first.

CHAPTER 23
THE THIRD DEATH

There was a third death, and it's the kind of secret I've never told anyone, not even myself, if you count the way I've pressed it down inside my skull like an old handkerchief packed with something you shouldn't ever, ever breathe.

Maybe this one's the worst of them. Maybe it's the only one that matters.

It didn't make the papers. I doubt it made a single authorized transcript or incident report, since technically, nobody involved had enough of a record to be missed.

The state would say there were no prisoners harmed, at least not the kind with case numbers and next of kin. It wasn't Dix, who only died twice, or Looper, whose death was performed for an audience that always looked away.

No, this one was a fifteen-year-old, a ward of nobody, a transfer.

I remember my first sight of the kid: rainy Thursday, coming off the elevator with his wrists handcuffed and his shoes in a plastic bag, just another intake but for how he looked at me, like he'd already solved something I was too stupid to understand.

He was so skinny the cuffs almost slipped right off, and his hair was the color of chicken fat, soaked flat to his head by the weather or maybe by whatever counted as discipline at the last stop.

The CO was pissed off, said the kid kept asking where they were taking him, so they parked him in the "prayer circle" and left him, less like a person and more like an unsorted package dropped in the wrong delivery bin.

He had the same nose as my brother, and the same long hands, and the same habit of always leaning toward the nearest exit as if mapping escape routes by instinct.

I had to check his transfer slip twice to make sure this wasn't some new cosmic punishment, some recursive joke the universe had queued up for me. The last name was different, but for a second, I couldn't let go of the feeling that it really was him, that my brother had grown up in another timeline and wandered through the walls of this place to haunt me for screwing up so much of my own life.

The kid didn't say anything that first hour, just sat with his knees locked together and his head down, fingers twisting at the hem of his orange jumpsuit.

I don't know why I did it, but when the time came for "chapel," I gave him the cup. It was a paper communion cup, the kind budgeted in bulk, and instead of actual grape juice it was filled with a corrections-issue powder drink that tasted like glue and antifreeze.

They called it "sacrament," but nobody cared if you shared it, as long as you didn't start a fight.

I handed it to him and said, "It helps," and he looked at me the way a stray looks at an outstretched hand, like he wanted to believe but knew some kind of trick was coming. He sipped it, and nearly spit it back out, but caught himself. He finished the cup, because that's what you do in jail; you finish what's handed to you, no matter how bad it burns.

Everything in this place is a test, and you only fail once.

We had barely finished the first hymn—a couple other sad sacks pretending to know the words—when the kid started making this low hum, like a phone buzzing against a wooden table. His body went rigid, eyes swimming for a second before both legs shot out and took the table with them.

The chair went, too, and his head snapped back against the wall hard enough to leave a dent. Somebody yelled "code," but the COs were slow, either because they didn't believe it or because some part of them thought kids this fucked up were better off dead.

I went to him fast, had to: he was convulsing, foam at the mouth, eyes wide open, but nothing behind them. For a split second, I thought he was faking, but the way he vibrated—like a trapped bird—told me different. I caught his head so it wouldn't bang off the floor again.

He looked at me, right in the face. "I don't want to," he said. Not "I don't want to die." Just "I don't want to." That was the last thing. His mouth kept moving, but it was just the leftover electricity pinging around his skull.

The med team took almost seven minutes to get there, and by then it was all over. You could feel the room drain out, the way a busted lightbulb kills a mood.

The CO in the room said, "Didn't see nothing," and everybody nodded because that's the only way anything ever gets done here.

I lifted the kid's body myself and helped get him to the gurney. The nurse asked, "Was this expected?" and I said, "Yeah." Because by then, it was.

I didn't write his name in the ledger. I didn't tell anybody, not even the night supervisor, who was too hopped up on Red Bull and self-loathing to care. They marked it as a medical incident and filed it under "prior condition." Nobody came to collect his belongings. I threw the shoes away.

I thought about asking the priest if there was some kind of prayer for kids like him. Instead, I just waited for everyone to file out and then I sat in the room with the lights off and told myself that it wasn't my fault, that whatever poison had shorted his system was planted long before he took the cup from my hand.

It helped, for about two minutes.

That was the night I stopped believing my own bullshit, but it took a year for the cracks to show. Some nights I'd wake up and see his face in the dark, stenciled in static on the wall, just staring at me and humming quietly. I wasn't the one who killed him, but I was the last one to look him in the eyes.

Tonight, when the voice says "two souls and yours," I think of him. I think maybe the count was wrong all along.

Maybe it's all me. Maybe that's why I'm here, in this house, counting down the hours until the next round. Maybe the whole point of purgatory is to watch yourself rack up the bodies, one dead kid at a time, until you finally see what you are.

CHAPTER 24
THE RADIO THAT SHOULDN'T EXIST

Nora isn't in this for salvation. She's not praying for angels, or for some bureaucratic thumb on the cosmic scales to tilt in her favor. Every step she's taken—the glances over her shoulder, the way her nails trace the seam of the linoleum, the carved initials under the window ledge in the basement rec room—has been about surviving another day, and making sure nobody else gets the drop on her before she can get the drop on them. She's in this for blood, and if she has to drag the entire system down with her, she'll do it to see if it screams.

After the second echoing ping—maybe a radiator, maybe something alive—she yanks me into the supply closet. Hard. Her fingers gouge deep into the meat of my upper arm, and if I look, I'll see bruises tomorrow.

I want to say something clever, but the only words I find are absolutely not clever, and so I swallow them. Inside, it's the stench of cleaning solvent and an old, wet mop. Our shadows jitter on the cinderblock from the swinging bulb, and there's dust coming off Nora's clothes like she's been exhumed.

Her face is inches from mine, her hair wild and half-shadowed. "Give me the fucking ledger," she hisses, her voice thin and spidery, like a wire about to snap.

"What ledger?" I say, but it's not a question, it's a reflex, and she knows it.

"Don't you dare lie to my face." She's not quite shouting, but her words come out bright and sharp, like she wants them to cut me. "I've watched you. You think nobody's paying attention, but I've seen you, every night for weeks, prying up that floorboard. You think you're clever? Those boards creak like bones. I counted twenty-three times. I even know which shoes you wear when you do it."

I consider shifting tactics, but there's nowhere to go in this closet. The only way out is through her.

"You have no idea what you're asking for," I say, and even I can hear how weak it sounds.

She leans closer, breath acrid, pupils blown. "I'm asking for proof," she says, a tremor in her voice that's a lot less fear and a lot more rage. "Of her. Of you. Every sick thing that's happened here. I'm not just going to sit around until it's my turn, or yours. I'm getting out or I'm burning it all down. That's my price."

I hold her gaze, and for a second, I think I see something other than hunger behind it—maybe the ghost of the kid she used to be, someone who believed grownups were supposed to keep you safe instead of feeding you to the machine. But it's only a second.

"You think some old trinkets and scribbled names will save you?" I say. "They'll eat you alive. They always do."

"I think they'll make people believe me," she says, teeth clenched so hard it's a wonder her jaw doesn't snap. "And I'll make damn sure your name is the first one they remember."

There's a sound from the hallway—a drag, a shuffle, something animal. Maybe just the janitor, or maybe the nurse. Or maybe it's Hale, come back early.

Adrenaline spikes. Nora doesn't blink. Her hand comes up, and now she's pressing something cold and sharp to my ribs—a little folding knife, probably stolen out of the art room supply box.

Her smile splits her face like a wound. "Hand it over," she

says, voice almost gentle, "or I go straight to the nurse. Let him dig it out of you instead."

The vent above us rattles, and I realize it's not just the two of us in the closet. The voice is back—the one that sometimes seeps out of the walls when you're too tired or too scared to sleep.

It's not a real voice, not exactly; it's more like the sound of teeth clicking together underwater, or a whisper through a mile of ductwork. But tonight, it's clearer than usual. It's hungry. It wants what Nora wants.

The voice in the vent laughs—a wet, greedy sound that makes the roots of my teeth ache and the hair along my collar stand on end. It's the kind of laugh you hear just before someone steps on your neck. I can't tell if it comes from Hale, or from the building itself, or maybe from whatever part of my brain was left to rot after last year. But whatever it is, it's feeding on us.

"You want it?" I say, and my voice comes out a little higher than I wanted. "Fine. But you're not going to like what you find."

"I already don't like what I found." She shifts the knife. "Where?"

"In my bag," I say. "Bottom pocket. The one with the safety pin."

She lowers the blade, but doesn't put it away. Her free hand snaps open my backpack, fingers digging past the tangle of broken pencils and stolen lighters and the half-melted candy bar I'd meant to eat at lunch. She finds the pocket, rips it open, and pulls out the ledger.

It's a dumb thing, really—a battered green spiral with half the pages missing, corners chewed by mice. But the things written inside aren't dumb. The names, the dates, the tally marks. The things that happened on certain nights, in certain rooms. Things that never made it to the nurse's log, or the police blotter, or anyone's memory except mine and, apparently, Nora's.

She flips it open, scanning past the first few pages. Her hands are shaking, but her face is stone.

"See?" I say, because it's all I have left. "It's just names. Just a bunch of dead kids and the idiots who didn't save them."

She looks up, and for the first time she seems to remember I exist. "There's more," she says. "There's always more."

She's right. The closet is smaller now; the vent is breathing, sucking us in. I can hear the voice in the wall, getting closer, licking its lips.

"You want to get out?" I say. "We have to go now."

Nora tucks the ledger under her arm, still holding the knife. "Lead the way."

We stumble into the corridor, which is a little too dark and a little too quiet, and the nurse is there, waiting at the end of the hall. His hands are clean, but his shirt isn't, and he's smiling like he knows what happens next.

The air is thick with bleach and something sweeter underneath.

The voice in the vent is louder now—echoing off the cinderblocks, sliding along the waxed tile. It's chanting, almost, repeating the same three words over and over until they stop meaning anything: "This. Is. Yours."

Nora takes a step forward, ledger clutched to her chest. "I'm not afraid of you," she says, but she's lying.

The nurse laughs. "You should be."

I know what comes next. I've seen it play out a hundred times, in a hundred rooms, with a hundred scared kids who thought they could outlast the system. But I'm not scared anymore. Not of the nurse, or the vent, or even of Hale.

I'm scared of Nora. And maybe that means I've already lost.

I make my move. I shove her hard, right into the nurse's arms, and for a second, they're both off balance.

The ledger goes flying, skittering down the hall. The nurse is fast—faster than he should be—but I'm faster. I grab the notebook and run, not looking back.

Behind me, I hear the vent start to scream.

I run for the exit, the pages fluttering in my hand, the names and the stories and the proof that none of us have ever really left this place. I run, and run, and run, and when the doors finally slam shut behind me, I realize I'm laughing.

I catch my breath, but it feels more like it catches me. I'm still not sure if I've outrun what's inside, or if I've just brought it with me.

The ledger is heavy in my hands, and I feel the weight of everything I didn't do. Everything I did. Nora's voice is in my ears, the way she said my name like a promise and a curse. I wonder how long it took her to stop screaming. How long I have until it's my turn again.

I keep laughing.

CHAPTER 25
THE DOOR ON THE NOT-FLOOR

Do you believe in hauntings? Most of them are real. Mine certainly are.

Let's talk about the circle.

The circle wasn't just a safe trick. It was my inheritance and my insurance, a binding agent for the wildness that sometimes seeped through the corners of wards like this, where the dying came to practice.

I'd learned about circles from my grandfather's brother, a veteran of three wars and countless clinics, who taught me in whispers about the difference between real and imagined hauntings.

"Sometimes," he'd say, "the line you draw is all that keeps you from learning the difference."

The hospital's power went out for the third night running, and things were happening in the dark that shouldn't have been.

A man lay on the floor at our feet, and his body seized up the moment the lights went out.

I grabbed anything I could and made a slap shift circle, tying myself, Nora, and a kid named Holland, into a makeshift ring around the guy on the floor.

We locked hands and chanted the old rhyme—half nursery,

half exorcism—while Nora counted the beats under her breath and the new kid, Holland, tried not to piss himself. Our hope was that the circle would hold, keep out whatever was knocking at the door to the world, or at least delay it until dawn.

But the circle wasn't supposed to break.

The rules had been clear: If you let go, you let it in.

Yet the circle around our feet broke and there was a snap, loud as a backfiring shotgun, and suddenly the noise in the room changed from ritual unity to riot.

Holland yelped and staggered away, hands still in fists, knuckles the color of boiled bone. Nora grabbed for him, whispering curses that made her sound more alive than I'd ever seen her, and the stair boss—old Rupe, who'd overseen the emergency stairs since the fifties—spat a black glob of tobacco juice on the linoleum and crossed himself so fast it was like he was trying to erase a memory.

Even the guy on the floor - the redhead, sudden and still—twitched, as if the violence of our panic briefly reminded his muscles how to work.

Around us the circle collapsed, not just in the physical sense but in the way the air got tight, the way the drafts reversed and started to pull in instead of out, as though the room had become a lung choking on its own breath. The hymn we'd started turned into a hiss, a snarl of syllables, as if the words themselves had curdled in the ambient fear.

I expected someone to start screaming, but what happened was worse: silence, the kind that falls when a roomful of people all realize at once that the enemy is inside the gates.

I scanned the faces: Holland's was already ruined, pupils blown wide as pennies in the blackout, sweat stringing down the sides of his jaw.

Nora, on the other hand, looked predatory, her lips skinned back from her teeth, eyes glittering with the kind of excitement that only comes from watching someone else's resolve fracture. She'd always been a collector of weaknesses—she cataloged the way people flinched at sudden noises, the way their hands trembled during blood draws, the way they avoided stories about dead children.

She was building a taxonomy of failure, and tonight, the specimen was me.

Behind her, Rupe slumped against the door, one hand clutching the lanyard with the emergency keys and the other jammed into his armpit, trying to keep his own heart in check. His lips moved in a prayer, but the only thing I could hear was the gurgle of Holland, retching quietly into the hem of his shirt.

In the middle of it all, the nurse with the composure—a woman in gray scrubs with the calm of a bomb technician—shouldered past the carnage and went straight to the inmate who was spasming.

Without hesitation, she stepped over the broken circle, not even glancing down at it. Her hands moved with precision, checking the carotid first, then peeling back an eyelid to see if there was anyone left behind the glass. The beads of sweat on her brow betrayed nothing, but I saw her jaw clench as she counted the pulse.

Three times she checked it, each time double- and triple-counting, because what she was feeling didn't make sense. The body should have been a corpse, blood pressure in negative digits, skin gone mottled and slack. Instead, the pulse throbbed steady and strong, as if someone had plugged him back in at the wall. For a second, the nurse just stared, caught in a logic trap, then looked up at me for confirmation.

I shrugged—I had no answers, only that the rules had changed, and we were now playing a different game.

That's when the light came back. Not the overheads—they stayed stubbornly dark, the cheap hospital bulbs flickering just enough to remind you of their absence. No, the light that returned was yellow and rotten, leaking out of the lamp on the side table in a way that made shadows crawl up the walls like desperate animals.

It shouldn't have been possible. The circuits had been cut, the breaker locked, and yet the lamp burned on, casting a nauseating lemon glow that made everyone's skin look jaundiced and sick. Our shadows fused together in a single dark web, impossible to untangle, whose limbs belonged to whom.

I swiped my tongue across my lips and tasted the familiar sting of blood, realizing I'd bitten down hard enough to open a vein inside my cheek. The taste was iron and salt and the memory of old bruises. It was a taste that belonged to the world outside the circle—the one that had just found its way in.

The nurse—older than she looked, probably seen more deaths than the stair boss—stood there, clutching the dying guy's wrist, head cocked as if listening for whispers in her veins. The lamp's light painted a sick halo around her, and in the sudden quiet, I could hear her breathing—a ragged, shallow drag, the sound a drowning person makes when they realize the surface is too far away.

I watched, transfixed, as a line of snot dripped from Holland's nose and splattered onto the floor, merging with blood from my own mouth. The nurse seemed to register the change in tempo; she raised her eyes, met mine, and for a second, we were the only two people in the room. She mouthed "Not possible," but the words never made it past her lips.

Then the vent in the ceiling moved.

It was the oldest trick in the building: if anything went wrong with the air, the vent would close, reset, and then open again, like a mechanical eyelid.

I'd seen it jam and grind, heard it scream when the bearings seized, but I'd never seen it move in total silence.

Tonight, it opened like an invitation, the cover sliding back to reveal the darkness beyond. Something in the air changed, a shift so subtle you had to be in the habit of hunting ghosts to feel it.

Every breath got heavier, tinged with the sour reek of ozone and antiseptic, the way the air tastes after a lightning strike. I felt the hairs on my arms rise, my skin crawling with an electric warning.

In the corner, Rupe stopped praying and just stared, mouth open, keys dangling from his fist. Nora, too, had gone quiet. Her predatory excitement melted to a sharp, queasy interest. Even Holland, hands still balled tight, lifted his head and squinted up at the vent, as if he expected something to come tumbling out.

The nurse was the first to move. She let the patient's wrist drop, wiped her hands on her scrubs, and stepped back just far enough to be outside the lamp's circle of light. Her eyes never left the vent. I edged closer to Nora, who didn't seem to notice, eyes locked on the ceiling.

The room was holding its breath, waiting for the next cue.

It came, inevitably, from the vent. A sound, faint at first, like a distant drill or a bee trapped in an empty soda can. Then, as the opening widened, the hum resolved into words—a kind of electronic voice, impossibly clear, like someone had wired a speaker into the ductwork and hidden it behind layers of dust and rat shit.

The words came in threes, digitized and inhuman: "Ledger due. Ledger due. Ledger due." Each repetition was louder, more insistent, echoing around the room until we were all forced to look up and face it.

I felt the sweat cool on my skin, a chill settling across my shoulders. Blood dripped from my cheek to the floor, and in the lamp's halo I watched it pool on the tile, round and perfect as a red coin. Holland whimpered, then clapped his hands to his ears. Rupe began to weep, and the nurse—her composure crumbling—took a single step backward, as if physical proximity could protect her from what was coming through the ceiling.

Nora, meanwhile, had a thin smile on her lips, the kind people get when they see something they never expected but always dreaded.

It whined open without a sound, and every eye followed the slow, mechanical slit as it yawned wider, exposing the ductwork and the blackness beyond. The nurse flinched back, but the hot nurse—the one with sailor tattoos and a silver tooth—leaned in, like she wanted to fall upward into the dark.

The vent should have been a passage for air, but tonight it was a mouth. The voice rolled out of it tinny and trilled, echoing off the Formica and the bone-dry cement, repeating what it had said before with the confidence of something that knew it had the room: "Ledger due."

The words felt cold, even though my body was sweating so hard I could see salt crusting in the crooks of my elbows.

Then, without warning, something knocked three sharp times under the floorboards, perfectly spaced, like a morse code for "you can't run."

The whole table jumped in unison.

The pretzel salt we'd laid in a line for luck trembled, and the little pile we used to mark the patient's name scattered itself into a crude star. The paper cups—three for water, one for bourbon—slid an inch toward the center of the table, as though an invisible hand had given them a push. No thread pulling. No trick rigged for that, not in this room. Not unless you counted the way desperation could move things.

I'd spent years in this place, learning its angles and its tells, and I knew you could fake tremors, you could fake voices, you could fake the sudden extinguishing of a candle. But you could not fake that kind of timing, not when it syncopated perfectly with your own pulse.

I felt my mouth go dry as the tongue of a cat, and realized I'd lost the thread entirely—lost the trick, lost the table, lost the entire fucking game to something that didn't even have the decency to show a face.

I heard, clear as glass, the chapel bell roll on the hour—once, twice—and in that moment the thread burned my fingers like a live wire, a static jolt that made me drop it onto the table.

It shriveled and curled away from me like a salted worm. The men gasped, and one of them—God bless his dumb bravado—crossed himself so hard he nearly punched his own jaw.

Nora laughed, a thin, reedy laugh that was worse than any scream, and I knew she'd be telling this story for weeks.

For the first time since I was nineteen, since the very first time I'd run a midnight session for the dying, I felt the bottom drop clean out of my trick. No more mirror. No more altar. No more clever sleight of hand to keep the wolves at bay. Just me, bare as a newborn, and a building that had learned my lines by heart and was now practicing them better than I ever could.

My stomach dropped, and a cold sweat ran up my back in a single wave, like I'd swallowed a snake made of ice. I felt—the only word for it is exposed, like something had stripped away my name and my skin and was now sniffing at the hollow underneath.

I tried to speak, but my tongue stuck to the roof of my mouth, helpless as a castaway.

CHAPTER 26
THE HATCH

I don't remember moving.

I don't remember crossing the distance, just that I'm standing in front of it, the circle behind me ruined.

But I'm standing in front of the hatch.

The hatch is nothing special, at least at first. The brass handle has been thumbed green by decades of dead hands. It's barely visible behind the peeling chartreuse paint, but the shape draws your eye.

Little architectural heresies like this are everywhere in the hospital, leftovers from moneyed eras when even the pneumatic infrastructure was built to impress.

Ask anyone and they'll tell you these tubes once ferried blood, stool, and body fluids from the upper floors to the mad scientists in the basement. Urban legend says one Christmas Eve in the 70s, a cigarette lighter rode the pneumatic down at the wrong moment, ignited pure oxygen, and turned the whole system into a pipe bomb.

I believe it. The scars on the walls don't lie.

Tonight, the hatch isn't just ornamental. It's the center of gravity, pulling at me with a pressure headache's insistence. The last thing I see before I touch the handle is the nurse, still hunched over the patient, picking at the waxed thread with a dental pick, bloodying her own fingers. Nora talks to the vent in a voice too small for her lungs, like she's praying to something in the duct-work. I can't tell if she's scared or ecstatic.

I twist the hatch open with a grunt. It sticks, then gives in a rush, the seal breaking with a breathy sigh. For a split second, I think the corridor itself is exhaling—like the whole building has been holding something in, and now it's letting go.

The air that pours out is cold, but not metallic or chemical like the morgue. It's the cold of open doors in the middle of winter, of forgotten stairwells and childhood cellars. It flows up, not down, and brings with it a note of ozone, distant woodsmoke, and something hot and faintly animal, like the scent of a predator's den after a kill.

Inside the hatch, cradled on the lip of the ancient metal chute, is a radio. Not a cell phone. Not a walkie. A fucking analog, military-green box, the kind with a rubberized push-to-talk and a rotary dial for frequency. My mind tries to tally up explanations but all of them sound like TV scripts: a prank, a plant, a misplaced antique.

Except the batteries are fresh and the red LED on the mic is on. Someone is transmitting, right now, on a line that shouldn't exist.

I glance over my shoulder. The nurse hasn't noticed. Nora has gone from whispering to humming, her breath misting in the chilly air. The patient's eyes are rolled back, all pupil, no iris. The circle looks like a chalk drawing on a blackboard after a class-room brawl—broken, trampled, and utterly inert. Whatever we were doing, it stopped mattering the second this radio showed up.

I reach for the box. My fingers tingle, not from static but from expectation, like the moment before you touch a doorknob that's been gathering charge all winter. Before I can even lift it out of the hatch, a bell rings.

Not the clatter of a nurse's station, or the polite chime of shift change—this is a cathedral bell, deep and slow and solitary, striking once from the bottom of a dry well. It vibrates the hatch in my hand, reverberates through the bones of my forearm.

And then, through the speaker, a woman's voice. Not clipped, not filtered—full, low, worn by cigarettes and years of night-shift arguments. It says, "Stop."

I freeze, every cell in my body turtling inward. The word is so gentle it feels personal, like a hand on your shoulder from behind when you're about to do something irreparable. It's not directed at me, but I know it's meant for me.

I don't stop. I pull the radio from the hatch, and as I do, the temperature in the corridor drops another five degrees. The bell rings again, closer now, and the voice—still soft, still knowing—says, "You shouldn't."

I thumb the transmit button and hear my own breath echo back a half-second later, doubled and slightly off, so it sounds like someone's standing beside me, breathing in tandem. I say, "Who is this?" and the speaker hisses, pops, and goes silent.

The air keeps moving. It rushes up the chute, brushes my cheek, and smells like burned rosemary and singed paper. The hatch slams shut behind me with a violence that feels personal, like a punishment. My hand still clutching the radio, I stumble backward, nearly tripping over the broken circle.

Nora gasps. "She's here."

The nurse finally looks up, her latex gloves scarred with blood and graphite. She sees me with the radio and for a moment every emotion—fear, envy, awe—plays across her face, like I'm holding a relic or a weapon. The patient starts convulsing, spittle foaming at the lips. In the commotion, the radio comes to life again, this time with nothing but white noise and intermittent, breathless laughter.

The hatch pulses. The metal shivers, as if something massive and restless is shifting behind it, just out of sight. The sound isn't mechanical, isn't wind—it's footfalls, slow and heavy, moving up the chute toward us. I back away step by step, feeling the chill wrap around my ankles like water rising in a flood.

At this point, my brain should be short-circuiting, but it's not. All I can think is: if this is a con, I'm not the one running it. For the first time in years, maybe ever, I'm not orchestrating the illusion—I'm just a mark, a spectator who wandered behind the curtain and found a live wire.

I close the hatch with a prayer and a kick. The corridor falls silent except for the wheeze of the patient's lungs and the soft, almost tender static from the radio. I want to drop it, smash it, but I can't. The heft of it in my hand feels like a promise, or a sentence.

For a long moment, I just stand there. Nora is crying, the nurse is muttering Hail Marys in a language I don't recognize, and the world outside the hospital—cars, city, streetlights—might as well be on another planet.

I think about all the times I've been told I was crazy, or that I was making it up, or that I was so smart I could talk myself into or out of anything. I think about how, even now, part of me is looking for the trick, the wires, the planted actors. Another part—the part that remembers the silence of other locked wards, and the way a voice can linger long after it should have died—knows it's real, or at least real enough.

The hatch doesn't open again. The radio grows heavier in my hand. The voice never comes back, but I hear it anyway, echoing in the ductwork and in the hollow of my ribs.

If you've never been gaslit by a building, you can't understand the feeling. It's like waking up in a dream where every detail is wrong, but you have to keep playing along because you forget the rules if you stop. You become the vessel, the conduit for every old secret and dead story that place has ever held.

I walk back to the patient, cradling the radio like a newborn. The nurse stares at me, waiting for instructions, but all I can say is, "It's over. For now." Nora wipes her eyes and nods, as if she's been expecting this ending all along.

The circle is broken. The air is colder, and the lights above us flicker with a rhythm that sounds almost like breathing.

I let the radio hang from my wrist and pretend I'm not shaking. I don't know who's haunting who anymore, but it doesn't matter. We're all just pieces in the same haunted machinery, and the only thing to do is keep moving until the gears grind you down.

This is what I think about while I wait for the sun to crawl back up the sky. The night is full of voices, but the loudest one is mine, telling myself to keep going, keep faking it, keep from falling apart.

It's almost comforting. Almost.

The night gets thin and brittle, like the membrane between waking and sleep, and for a while nothing happens. The nurse cleans up, Nora disappears to her own shadows, and I sit in the corridor with the radio on my lap, thumb tracing the rotary dial. I want to call out, to ask the voice who it is, what it wants. But I know the answer already.

The bell will ring again, someday soon. The hatch will open, and something will come up to meet me. Until then, I wait. And when it does, I'll be ready.

CHAPTER 27
THE SECOND RADIO

JACK

One minute, the light was on. Next, it's gone. I hear nothing. No shuffles, no breathing other than my own. Simply nothing.

But when the light comes back on, Cole is gone.

Fucking gone.

The emoji I text to Ike is just a bell, but he reads it like a sentence.

He shows up in ten, hands jammed in jacket pockets, boots ringing the steel stairs with a sound that's half warning, half resignation.

We don't do omens solo; that's just asking to be anthropomorphized by something old and patient. So we team up, always, even when the bell is for someone else.

He takes one look at Jasper, who was standing outside the door, and says, "So it's a bell night," with less surprise than expected.

"Guy disappeared the second the light went out," I tell him as I hand him my backup headlamp, the one with the logo melted off in a microwave accident. He straps it on backward, like an idiot, then flips it around and gives me a lopsided grin. He gestures to the thermos I'm cradling like a talisman and says, "Is that coffee?"

"Better," I say. "It's bourbon, so if we die, at least our blood will burn."

He tilts his hand, an old toast. "Walk me through."

I point to the corridor, the floor, the chalk lines that look like a madman's attempt at hopscotch. "He made a circle," I say. "Pretzel salt perimeter. Red thread to the vent. Paper cups from the dispenser in the rec room. Pastor Cole is talking like he wants salvation to sign for a package. Building answered."

Ike's eyebrows go up. "Building answered how?"

I gesture at the lingering ozone in the hall, at the way the air tastes like tinfoil and confession. "Ask Casper."

Casper, to his credit, is regaining speech. "Pastor was praying into the vent. The light flashed. No one's supposed to be in that wing. No power to the panel since Easter."

Ike's eyes flick to the ceiling, the ductwork. "So the vent's acting like a confessional. And the building's listening."

I shrug, but my nerves are doing their own relay. "I believe in radios," I say, "but the radio Cole wedged in the duct was dead when I pulled it. No battery, no wire. Still, the call bulb blinked. And not just once—like it was tapping out a code."

Ike grins. "The HVAC system is haunting us."

"Maybe," I say. "Or someone is using the duct as a relay."

He nods, files it away. "All right. We check the line. You got the scanner?"

I pass him the battered police-band handheld, still warm from my pocket. He flips it on, thumbs through frequencies until a low, harmonic hum fills the space between us.

We move out—old maternity corridor, abandoned since they put up the new wing in the seventies. The wallpaper's peeling off, but the ghosts never bothered to update. Dust on the tiles makes a dry applause with every step. This is the part where you keep your hands where you can see them, because the stuff in these halls doesn't like surprise guests.

Ike slows at the nurses' station and points his headlamp at the counter. There—heel marks in the flour-fine dust, not inmate boots, not even the cheap slip-ons they give the orderlies. These are small, quick, and pivoting toward the wall like the walker changed direction when the bell rang.

"Not a patient," he says.

"Staff," I confirm, and he nods. We both know this means trouble.

We split the room: he checks the junction box on the left, and I take the pneumatic hatch on the right. The hatch is old brass, cold enough to bite. I lever it open and shine my light inside. The duct's throat is black, but something glints about a meter in. I fish it out with a telescoping magnet. It's another radio, newer, sleeker, batteries still taped in. The mic is live, little red LED blinking like it knows we're watching.

Ike leans in. "Somebody's broadcasting?"

I turn the radio in my hand. "Not ours. Not theirs either." I point to the sticker on the back. "Brand new. No dust. No dust beard means it's been serviced."

He steps back, makes a face. "So our ghost has a handler."

I kill the radio, but the silence is instantly shredded by a bell ping, clear and sharp, somewhere lower in the ducts. Ike's lips move, nearly a prayer, then he snaps it shut before the word can finish.

"Someone's in the sub-basement," he says. "Or something else is."

"Could be a loose clapper in the plumbing, pretending to be church," I offer.

Ike smirks, but it's all teeth. "Yeah. And maybe Matron Hale retired to Tampa."

We search. I've got the little screwdriver from my kit.

Floorboards at the far end of the corridor make a hollow sound under my foot, so I drop and start working the seam. The board lifts after two tries, and there's a notebook inside, ledger-thick. Old. Smells like paste and mothballs.

The first ten pages are neat, with patient names in columns and discharge signatures at the end of each line. Then the handwriting changes. The new pen is heavier, more desperate. Under October entries, there's a Halloween page with an extra name, then a gap—no signature, no finish, just the pen trailing off the edge of the paper. Like the writer had to choose between finishing the letter and breathing.

I set the ledger on the tile. Ike crouches next to me, but doesn't touch. We've learned to let haunted objects set their own terms.

"You ever think the floor's got a better memory than we do?" he says.

I don't answer. I don't need to.

He flicks the headlamp off, then on. "You're writing this up?"

"I'm writing it down," I say. "What happens after that is up to administration."

He snorts. "Yeah, and administration is just where truth goes to get folded into smaller and smaller shapes."

"Then we'll unfold it later," I say, and slip the ledger into my bag like I'm pocketing a sick relative's keepsake. This is how we keep the world predictable: we treat the impossible with paperwork.

We head back. At the corner of the corridor, the call bulb blinks again. Once. Twice. Then nothing. I stop and look at the wiring bundle with a frown.

"Emergency could be bleeding power," Ike offers.

"Or the building's got muscle memory," I say.

"Or somebody downstairs thinks they're a saint," he says, and we both smile like it's a joke, but it's not.

We look at each other. In that look is a promise: if things go south, we'll make sure it's the right people who take the hit.

Cole is back and waiting at the circle, red thread marks around his wrists. He's been pulling at them, slow and steady, the way you test fences. Nora is with him, standing with her arms crossed and that satisfied calm you get after a successful petty theft.

"You found her book," Nora says, voice sharpened by triumph.

I hold it up, ambiguous. "Found a book."

"Same difference," she says, and she's already planning how to spend the win.

Cole isn't looking at us. He's staring at the vent, face hollowed out by the light. "I didn't put that radio there," he says.

"I know," I reply, and for some reason he crumples a little more.

He looks at me. I mean really looks, like a man in a confessional who's just realized the priest is the same guy who bullied him in gym class thirty years ago. "I want to finish," he says. "For the record."

"Then talk," I say. "You've got five minutes."

He breathes like a condemned man. "Thank you, Brother Jack," he says, and this time there's no honey or sarcasm in it.

He looks at the vent like it's a hung jury. Then at me, like maybe I'm the only one who'll remember this right.

"I killed a boy," he says. "Not with my hands. With my belief. With my performance dressed like belief. They told us if we confessed every day, there'd never be a secret left to rot. But I held one back. For ten years, I pretended it was just a hard night, a fluke. Tonight, the building counted him for me."

He gives me two names we both know, then the one he's never said aloud.

Somewhere in the ducts, the bell rolls a long, metallic note, then sags into silence. The vent exhales like a sigh.

"Ledger due," the speaker says, as if it's been waiting for this cue all night.

Ike steps in. "You hear that?"

"Unfortunately," I say.

Nora smiles at the vent like it's a mirror finally returning her gaze. "She likes you," she says, and I resolve to never be liked by ghosts again.

"Time," I say, because if we don't get Cole back to his cell soon, somebody's going to come looking. And the last thing we need is another body to hide.

CHAPTER 28
THE WARDEN'S ASK

The Warden is waiting before the elevator has finished breathing open, exactly as I would have bet, tie already loosened, smile ironed and creased in the corners as if he practiced it daily in the reflection of a butter knife or the building's chrome fixtures.

Some men are their own audience; he's the kind who checks his expression in every passing shine as if his face is evidence to be preserved. Our elevator doors provide a full-length mirror, and he uses them.

"I thought I heard activity up here," he says, voice pitched just below echo as if he's allergic to the sound of his own authority repeated back at him. There's a sharpness to his consonants, a warning that he'd rather be asleep, or dead, than chasing ghosts in his building on Halloween night.

"Storage disturbance contained," I say, which is true in the way that duct tape is a medical device and a locked trunk is a coffin. The blood has been mopped but the trail is still wet in memory, the residue of what happened not so much erased as disguised. We're all experts at that here.

He gives a slow, ascending nod, like he's checking off a list. "And no, ah, escalation?" His glance flicks between me and Ike, lingering in the negative space between us, as if the silence might confess where our mouths won't.

I take the second radio from my pocket, now sealed in the kind of clear plastic bag they use for evidence or sandwiches, and lay it in his open hand. The fingers curl around it like the jaw of a trap, slow but certain. His mouth does something almost imperceptible —a twitch that's not surprise but a kind of predatory arithmetic. He weighs the radio like a gold coin, then lifts it up in the ambient light, as if expecting it to whisper someone's name.

"Off the books?" he asks, not quite a question, more of a suggestion with teeth.

"Depends on the book," I say, and watch his eyes for the glint of understanding. I can tell the exact moment he registers I'm holding something else in reserve. The ledger in my satchel is the size and weight of a brick, and it pulses like a second heart. I wonder if he can hear it.

His smile restructures, becomes more economic. "And where was this?" he asks, holding the radio with two fingers, like a relic he doesn't want to contaminate.

"Pneumatic hatch on sublevel B," I say, and Ike grunts in confirmation, though I can't tell if it's solidarity or the aftershock of what he just witnessed. The Warden accepts this with another of his slow-motion nods, calibrating new variables in his head.

"Maintenance has been, ah, inconsistent," he says finally, each word measured like medication. We both know what he's really saying: Some janitors are cheaper than others, and all of them are ghosts before they're even out the door.

Ike says nothing, which is his special skill—he can weigh a silence, measure its temperature, and adjust accordingly. The Warden notices, and for a second it looks like he's about to ask Ike something, but the moment passes and he files the silence away for later.

"Cole confessed," I say. "On the record." I let the ambiguity coil between us. I don't mention the rest. I don't mention that I recognized the look in Cole's eyes—the way the pupils flatten when you're already halfway to the other side and the only thing keeping you here is the memory of a promise you made to nobody.

"Good," the Warden says, too fast, as if the word burned his tongue on the way out.

"And there's an older log," I say, "in the hatch. Pre-merger ledger." I can feel the temperature in the hallway drop twenty degrees. The Warden's eyes snap to my bag, then back to my face, then to the radio, like he's triangulating the location of a mine.

He lowers his voice. "Jack," he says, using my name like a scalpel, "you know how we handle… artifacts."

I smile. "With gloves. Slowly. And with plausible deniability."

His own smile becomes an isometric exercise. "Discreetly," he says, voice barely more than a breath. "And anything found in storage is property of the facility."

"People are property of the facility too," I remind him, "and they keep leaving."

For a split second, his mask slips, and there's a tic near his jaw —a miniature earthquake. "Don't get pious with me," he says, and now there's an edge, a challenge, a half-remembered rivalry.

"You brought me here for piety," I say. "Or the appearance of it."

He stares at me for a long time, and I wonder which of us will blink first. I know his type: cultivated in crisis, promoted by attrition, educated by the laws of what-you-can-get-away-with. He's considering whether to threaten or flatter. Eventually, he chooses expediency wrapped in the cellophane of trust.

"I need a clean report," he says. "No radios. No old paperwork. Write up the incident as a routine disturbance, with no staff involved and no patient access. Just a service interruption."

"Staff involvement," I repeat, rolling the phrase on my tongue like a bitter pill. "So you already know who planted the second radio."

He doesn't blink. That's the tell. "It's better if this ends with us," he says. "Rumors hurt people. Reputations. Careers."

"Sometimes rumors save people," Ike says, and it's the first time he's spoken since the elevator. His voice is neutral, but his hand is clenched around the battered handle of his thermos. The Warden regards Ike for the appropriate duration—enough to register his presence, not enough to dignify it.

"I do appreciate your diligence," he tells Ike. "Your, ah, restraint. I will make sure it's noted." The politeness is a velvet glove over a garrote.

I slide the ledger deeper into my bag, zipping it shut hard enough that the zipper's finality echoes down the hall. The Warden hears it and his eyes flick up, then down, then away. I say, "I'll file the report."

"Thank you," he says. The smile is back, automatic now, like a default setting after a system crash. "Tonight, if possible?"

"I write better when the building's still breathing," I say.

He gives that slow, ambiguous nod again, and I notice a tremor in his fingers as he pockets the radio, the plastic bag catching the light like a fresh body tag. The elevator pings behind him.

Before he steps inside, he says, "Happy Halloween, Jack."

"It is," I say, and mean it. Halloween is the one night this building feels honest, the one night when the rules of the living don't quite apply, and the staff can pretend the dead are just costumes and not unfinished business.

The doors swallow him whole.

Ike leans against the wall and lets out a laugh that's been shaken down to its bones. "That man," he says. "He doesn't even know what he's scared of."

"Everyone's scared of something," I say, "even if it's just the paperwork."

He grins, a little less haunted than before. "You keeping the book?"

"Borrowing," I say. "Long-term."

Ike nods, arms folded over his chest, and the corridor feels smaller, safer, like the two of us could hold it against the rest of the world if we had to. There's a kinship in secrecy, a camaraderie in the lies you're forced to keep.

"What's your plan?" he says, voice pitched low.

"Read it," I say. "And decide if I'm a nurse, or a priest."

He looks at me for a while, mouth quirked like he's trying on different responses. Finally, he says, "Be both. Hand out absolution in pill cups."

A line so good I'd hug him for it, if we were that kind of friends.

Instead, I pour a finger of coffee from my battered thermos into the cap and offer it to him. "Communion," I say.

He takes it, raises it in a silent toast, and drinks.

"Amen."

CHAPTER 29
THE BUILDING ALWAYS TELLS THE TRUTH

I write tonight in the dead center of the break room, my thermos open and steaming, the door propped not with a stopper but with my left foot—a gesture of détente to whatever's making the rounds in this building besides us.

There's a theory that Halloween thins the air, that the boundaries between the living and whatever else are as cheap and porous as the cheesecloth they use for ghosts in prison crafts. I believe it. You can hear more when oxygen behaves like that — when it leaks and lets in extra channels. I keep an ear tuned for the building, but mostly I write.

First, the report: I drafted it clean and tight, all in the official style. My job is to make events seem routine, to blunt the sharp edges so management doesn't sprain their minds.

"Disturbance contained. Ritual paraphernalia confiscated. Inmate Ephraim Cole offered confession; names recorded and forwarded to appropriate authorities. No injuries." My report will make no mention of radios that buzzed on dead frequencies, or ledgers that bled ink into the grain of the page, or bells that rang where no bell ought to be.

Bells, here, are not equipment—they're punctuation. Sometimes even grammar.

The other document—the one that matters—fills my personal notebook. I write out the names given by Cole in a trembling block caps, then again in the long, looping curse-script they teach you to respect in Catholic school. I underline them, once for each time I heard them repeated in the vent.

I transcribe the ledger's last page in excruciating detail, careful to copy the unfamiliar marks and the numbers that aren't part of any official census. I sketch the pivot points of the heel marks on the not-floor, the way they radiated outward from the hatch, like dancers caught mid-flinch. I note the nurse-call bulb's two blinks at 01:23, the single, childish blink at 02:07. And I draw the hatch. This time, I add a label: "second radio, unknown handler."

Ike watches, not reading, just observing the act of writing the way you'd watch someone suture their own wound. He's chewing a pen cap and glancing at the clock every ten minutes, like he's waiting for a verdict. I wonder if he thinks we'll get an extra hour tonight, or if the clocks will skip us on purpose. I wonder if it matters.

"You think Hale was real?" he asks finally, not looking up from the wall he's been pretending to inspect for cracks.

I shrug. "I think institutions are haunted by the things they call programs. They invent a name, and then it wants to eat."

He nods at that, the way you nod when the riddle fits but the answer is still ugly. "And tonight?"

"Tonight, we fed it." I close my notebook, thumb the edge where the pages leave a faint line on my palm. "Or it fed us. I haven't decided."

He points with his chin at the old book in my bag. "You keeping that in your locker?"

"For now." I meet his eyes. "Books like that don't take to basements."

We do the last round together; it's an unspoken tradition for nights like this, so no one walks the building alone, and then, without saying a word, we both head to my office.

We sit in silence, as if a question had been spoken and we're waiting for someone to respond. After five minutes, a bell answers. Faint, maybe only imagined, but insistent the way a toothache is insistent.

"Ledger due," the wall murmurs, or maybe it's just the pipes, but the pipes here have too many opinions.

"Got it," I say, not to Ike but to the place—let it believe I'm still the obedient child it raised.

I look to Ike and see the answer already there —a shared secret. He says nothing. Some things are better left unsaid; some debts are easier to pay that way.

I pour a last inch of black coffee into my cup, swirl it until the dregs form a shape that's somewhere between an "O" and a closed loop. That feels about right. I think about the ledger, Cole's deal with the wall, and how Nora chewed her carrot sticks as if she were angry at the orange. I think about the warden and his joke about Halloween, the radio that wasn't there, and the hands that wrote the extra entry in the ledger—whether they were attached to a body or just the idea of one.

The building breathes.

So do we, for now.

Most nights I listen to men who lie because it helps them live longer.

On Halloween, you listen to the building; you let it tell its story. What it kept, what it spent, who it counted, who it didn't. The difference between a haunted house and a prison is just the paperwork.

I close my notebook, snap the elastic band, leaving a welt on my thumb. That's a form of punctuation, too. The ledger in my bag is heavier than it should be. I wonder if that's a trick of the mind, or if every name you add gives it heft. I wonder what happens when it gets too heavy to carry.

I text Ike a single emoji—🎃—because in the old stories, candle pumpkins were lanterns for lost souls. He replies with a bell. We're even.

When the morning crew comes in, the thirteenth floor will stop existing again. They'll look for a cup, a pen, a shift log, and find none. That's fine. People need their favorite holidays and their favorite lies. I'll file what I file. I'll keep what I keep. I'll wait to see who comes to ask for the ledger and whether they know the right name to say at the door.

And if the wall whispers again, I'll answer.

That's my job.

And on Halloween, it's my privilege.

LIGHTS OUT ON 13

The chapel lights are never supposed to be this bright. Fluorescent hum so high it sounds like teeth grinding.

Cole's chair sits dead-center beneath the cross, empty except for the red thread coiled on the floor like a vein cut short.

I'm not the first one here.

Casper stands near the altar, pale and rigid, his hands clasped behind his back. For a second, I think he's praying—until he turns, and I see the tremor in his jaw, the way his eyes flick not at me but to the far pew.

"Jack," he says, voice thin. "He's gone. Cole. They said you signed him out."

"I didn't sign anything," I tell him.

But he's already shaking his head, and that's when I see it: the ink stamp on his wrist. Clearance seal. Admin level.

The doors creak behind me.

The Warden steps in like a sermon that's been waiting for its cue. Clean shirt, perfect knot in his tie, eyes that never fully close. He looks from me to the empty chair, to the thread still warm on the tiles.

"Evening, Jack," he says. Calm. Polite. The kind of tone

bureaucrats use when they're already writing the report. "You shouldn't be here."

"Neither should he," I say, nodding at Casper.

The Warden smiles the way a file cabinet might—hinges tight, all edges. "Officer Casper is assisting with records management. Temporary reassignment."

Casper doesn't move. Doesn't blink. His eyes track the floor, and I see it—just for a second—his reflection in the polished tile isn't matching the angle of his body. A trick of the light, maybe. Or the building showing me who's really running things.

The Warden steps closer, folds his hands. His tie is straight, not a wrinkle on him. "The tape from your office," he says. "It's missing. Entire sequence of your shift—gone from the system. You understand how delicate these incidents can be."

"Gone?" I ask. "I told you Cole confessed. It's on that recording."

He tilts his head. "We reviewed a copy before it was pulled. You did good work, Jack. Sometimes, though, a confession is worth more *forgotten* than filed."

I feel the air tighten between us, that sterile, chemical kind of silence the hospital specializes in.

He lowers his voice. "Consider it handled."

He bends, picks up the red thread, winds it slowly around his finger. "Some stories are safer unspooled."

Casper's breath hitches. His reflection twitches again, like it's still trying to catch up.

I should walk out. I should let them finish whatever cleanup they've started. But the chapel smells like bleach and burnt copper, and I know the Matron's ledger doesn't balance itself.

"You ever hear bells, Warden?" I ask.

He glances at me, half amused. "Only when it's time to change shifts."

The thread tightens around his finger until the tip turns white. Then—softly, unmistakably—a single chime echoes through the vents overhead.

Casper flinches. The Warden doesn't.

He tucks the thread into his pocket. "Goodnight, Jack. Get some rest."

When I turn back to the altar, Casper's gone. No sound. No footsteps. Just the faint smell of ozone and the impression of his shape burned into the air like a flashbulb afterimage.

I'm alone with the cross and the hum.

The chapel light flickers once, twice, and steadies.

I pick up my recorder, press the red button, and whisper, "For the record—there's always a thirteenth floor."

Then the bell rings again, closer this time.

FINAL NOTE

They say the building sleeps once the lights go out. They're wrong. It just listens.

A few nights after everything that happened on the thirteenth floor, I found this tucked inside the Matron's old ledger. The paper was brittle, with scorched edges. The signature's faded, but the hand—neat, confident, almost motherly—is hers. **Matron Margaret Hale.**

Maybe she wrote it before the fire. Maybe the fire wrote it through her. Hard to tell with this place.

The Warden would've ordered it destroyed, but the file landed on my desk instead, right on top of my shift report: no return address, no routing tag. Just a single line scrawled across the envelope: *"Census complete. Steward confirmed."*

I've read it a dozen times. Each time the vents seem to breathe a little deeper. Each time, the bells in the chapel ring once more than they should.

So, before you leave these halls—before you shut the lights—remember: Every name gets written down somewhere. Every nurse eventually hears their own.

And the Matron? She's still keeping count.

THE LAST RITUAL NIGHT: THE STEWARD'S CENSUS

(Found in the Night Log, Entry Unnumbered)

I. Routine

They told me the night shift was easy—keep an eye on the monitors, log the rounds, don't piss off the nurses. That was two months ago.

Now I'm alone on Halloween night, sitting in Security B, watching twenty-four screens filled with nothing but stale hallways and the occasional flicker of light from the chapel. Someone put a candy bowl on the counter. The wrappers move on their own every time the vents sigh.

My name's **Ethan Shaw**, security trainee. Technically, I'm not supposed to be here alone, but the supervisor called in sick. "Nothing ever happens up there anymore," he said. "That floor's sealed."

He meant the **North Wing**. He meant the floor that doesn't exist.

Ward C was shut down years before I started. The maps skip from twelve to fourteen. But there's still an entry for *M-13* in the digital system. If you try to delete it, the computer says *Access Denied – Matron User Active.*

147

I thought that was a joke—a bug. Now I'm not so sure.

At 11:59 PM, every screen on the monitor wall glitches. Just static, like snow falling over old footage. Then one camera clears —a stairwell feed. And standing at the bottom step is a man in scrubs, back to the camera. Clipboard in hand. **Badge ID: J. STEEN.**

I rub my eyes. The badge isn't even active in the system anymore. But the timestamp on the screen says **NOV 1, 03:00 AM.** Three hours from now.

The radio crackles.

"Census commencing. All staff please confirm attendance."

The intercom hasn't worked in years. But the voice is calm, low, professional. A nurse's voice. And it knows the protocol.

II. The Glitch

00:14 The power dips. Only for a second, but long enough to feel the dark *lean in.*

The hallway lights return in sequence: east wing, west wing, chapel, morgue. Then, from somewhere above, a single bell rings.

The system console flashes a notification: **AUDIT RUN: CENSUS_13 – BEGINNING CYCLE.**

I try to cancel the process. No response. The cursor locks. Every camera feed changes to the same hallway—long, window-less, too narrow to belong anywhere in this building. The time-stamp scrolls backward, numbers running like someone rewinding a clock until it breaks.

Through the grain, I can make out figures. Dozens of them, walking single file, heads down, hospital gowns fluttering. They don't look at the camera, but one raises a hand as if to mark the count. The monitor logs *1, 2, 3…*

I check the system log. The name "HALE, MARGARET" scrolls by under *User Access*. Then another: "STEEN, JACK." And then mine: "SHAW, ETHAN – PERMISSION GRANTED."

I try to log off. The keyboard types by itself.

PRESENT.

The word repeats until it fills the screen.

III. The Stairwell

00:33. The radios on every floor turn on at once. A quiet hum— a 440Hz tone that shakes the teeth in my skull. The old-timers used to say the building had a "heartbeat frequency." Now I know what they meant.

I grab my flashlight and leave the office. The stairwell smells like bleach and burnt paper. Every third step creaks as if someone's walking ahead of me, always just out of sight.

At the landing between twelve and fourteen, the numbering skips—as expected. But tonight, there's a new sign bolted into the wall.

M-13: STAFF ACCESS ONLY.

It's not dusty. It's brand new. The bulb above the door flickers, revealing a smear of red thread caught around the handle.

I tell myself it's just a prank. Still, I open the door.

IV. The Floor That Shouldn't Be

The hallway stretches longer than geometry should allow. Pale green tile. No windows. The air feels like standing in someone else's dream.

A clipboard lies on the floor. Top page: *LEDGER – STAFF CENSUS, 2025 EDITION.*

The first name: **Margaret Hale.** The second: **Jack Steen.** The third: blank.

My flashlight sputters and steadies. There's a figure halfway down the corridor. A man in scrubs, shoulders hunched, pen tapping against a clipboard. "Sir?" I say. "You're not supposed to be down here."

He doesn't answer. He turns slightly, enough that I see the outline of his badge. **STEEN, J.**

"Mr. Steen?" I whisper. "You—"He raises a hand for silence,

then gestures to the clipboard in my grasp. His voice, when it comes, is quiet and patient.

"All staff must confirm attendance."

My throat dries. "I'm not staff," I manage. He looks past me, toward the door I came through.

"You are now."

The vents open with a sigh, exhaling cold breath across my neck. A faint hum vibrates the walls, spelling something that feels like counting.

One. Two. Three. Present.

The clipboard in my hand fills in its own line: **SHAW, ETHAN – CONFIRMED.**

At the end of the hall, the man nods once, satisfied. Then he sets down his pen, tucks the ledger under his arm, and steps backward into the wall. Not *through* it. *Into* it—like the wall was built around him and just remembered its mistake.

V. Reconciliation

03:00 AM. The vents ring a soft bell tone. Once. Then silence.

When I wake, I'm sitting at the security desk. The monitors are clear. The power steady. No alarms. On the counter, the candy bowl is full again. The wrappers are folded into perfect little shapes—tiny hospital bells.

I check the system log. Last night's entry ends with a single note:

CENSUS COMPLETE – ACCOUNT BALANCED.

Under signatures, one name: **STEWARDSHIP CONFIRMED: J. STEEN.** And underneath, in handwriting that is mine but not quite, smaller: **ASSISTANT STEWARD: E. SHAW.**

When I look up, the hallway camera shows the stairwell door slowly closing on its own. A faint, rhythmic echo drifts through the speakers. Three beats. Pause. One.

I whisper into the empty room, just to see if the building's still listening: "Present."

The vents answer, softly.
Account received.

The census never ends—only the counters change.

THE NURSERY FLOOR

It's been a week since the thirteenth floor stopped pretending it doesn't exist.

It's been a fucking shit show ever since. Believe it or not, I don't care, but every night at 03:00, the annunciator tree blinks red on a floor that shouldn't have power.

The maternity ward has been sealed since 1974 and yet the vent over my desk just whispered, *"Prepare the delivery."*

I'll log it like everything else.

22:37 —

North Wing's quiet. Even the chapel's behaving. Casper's replacement is making too much coffee in Security; I can smell it through the vents, like burnt toast, every time the fans kick on.

Warden's memo says ignore the phantom light on the *maternity level* if it pings again. *Sealed since '74. No access. False alarms common.*

Sure. Our false alarms cry.

22:41 —

There it is. Red diode blinking on the old annunciator tree—the one they were "definitely going to remove." I note it on the log, radio Ike, get nothing but hiss tuned to a heartbeat. The hiss hums a lullaby I haven't heard since we lost Mrs. Fen. Not a hymn. A nursery song. Four notes rising, two falling. The exact shape a mother makes out of breath and hope when she wants luck to keep its promises.

22:45 —

Warden texts: *Stand down. You're not cleared for that floor.*

I text back a thumbs-up lie and pocket the recorder.

22:51 —

Elevator. The panel refuses to remember thirteen. The panel always refuses polite untruths. I key fourteen, ride in the hum of wires and regret. On the way, the car stutters between floors with the tired sigh of a body deciding whether to keep living.

The doors open onto a corridor I don't know.

No sign. No windows. No security dome.

Tile the color of baby milk.

The smell hits first—old milk sweetening, iodine, talc, the distant ghost of something cleaner than we deserve. You don't forget that smell if you've worked any cradle unit. It's the smell of a room that expects a person who doesn't know what a room is.

I step out. The elevator changes its mind and tries to close. I keep my hand on the door until it gives up and sulks open again. I want an escape that can find me when I ask.

A callboard hangs beside a door with frosted glass. *NURSERY* is etched backward on the other side. The bulbs in the board are dead except one—red, steady, pulsing. Above it, a paper label curls: **DELIVERY 3.** No other numbers. Just the third of something that never had one or two.

"Who's playing," I say to the empty hallway, "and why on my shift?"

The vent answers by inhaling. The lullaby threads through—metal throat singing to itself.

I take the recorder out anyway. I press red.

"Nursery floor. False alarm. If I don't come back, burn this and tell the Warden I said something clever."

No one laughs.

The door opens when I touch it. No handle. It opens skin-warm the way mouths do.

Inside: a wall of cribs.

White enamel legs, chipped, mattresses thin as some last kindness.

Thirty? Forty? More. Most draped in gauze veils tied in bows yellowed by decades. The gauze moves though the air doesn't.

My name is chalked on a slate by the counter where bottles used to line like soldiers: **STEEN – NIGHT.** It's written in a hand I don't use unless I'm pretending to be patient.

The lullaby drops an octave. Mobiles spin above three cribs that don't have dust. Stars and moons cut from paper. In the motion, I see the shadow of a hand that isn't there, keeping time.

The intercom crackles. A woman's voice—brisk, gentle, Ruthless in the way kindness has to be if it wants to survive a hospital —speaks three words I didn't know I missed.

"Prepare the delivery."

"I'm not OB," I tell the ceiling. "I'm graveyard."

The ceiling hisses like a smile that doesn't include the eyes.

On the counter: a chart on a metal clipboard. The cover is clean. Crisp. The ink is wet enough my finger comes away pink when I touch the signature line.

PATIENT: HALE, MARGARET
ROOM: DL-1
STATUS: ACTIVE LABOR
FETAL HR: —
ATTENDING: STEEN, J.

I look for the joke, as a courtesy. No joke offered. Just another page. My name again, typed this time, under **FATHER/CONTACT.** The hospitals we inherit always have more information than we volunteered.

"Yeah," I say, "funny."

The door to Delivery looks like it was painted yesterday. The strip of viewing glass shows nothing, which in a hospital means everything is deciding what to be.

I push in.

—

Delivery rooms all look the same when you take the color away: too much white, a table that hopes to look like a bed, a light that believes in miracles because it's paid to. This one kept its props but lost its audience. Metal stands without tags. Towels without date stamps. A form in the waste bin that says *FILED* in red letters no one uses anymore.

On the table, under the sheet, a shape attends to breathing with discipline. The sheet hides enough to let you think this is modest. The sheet is a liar.

I say her name because names keep rooms from making their own. "Matron Hale."

The sheet lifts at the sternum like breath is a wave. Then it settles. The monitor on the wall wakes up, displays two lines that begin to speak to each other.

Top line: **120** bumps per minute, quick as a sparrow.

Bottom line: **74** slowing, a heart deciding it can afford to.

"Don't," I tell the machines. "Not tonight."

The intercom clicks. No voice. Just a pencil on paper somewhere behind it, moving without a hand.

The chart automatically switches to the next page.

PROCEDURE: Induction completed.

OUTCOME: Pending.

NOTES: *Balance requires replacement.*

A contraction wrings the air tight. The sheet clenches and releases. There's a sound straddling two possibilities—pain and relief. If you've worked births, you know both wear the same face in the middle.

I've worked deaths. It's the same music, different tempo.

"Okay," I say, because I am the adult and the adult doesn't show his fear. "Okay."

I glove. I don't know why. I know why. We put on gloves when we want to pretend we aren't touching the thing that makes us what we are.

The metal tray beside the table holds instruments, all wrong in a way my brain can't name without letting me use them. The forceps curve like questions I won't answer. The scissors have a nick on one blade that looks like a bite mark.

The lullaby slows. Whoever is singing has sat down. Whoever is singing knows this song's last verse.

"Breathe," I say, to everyone in the room. The room obeys. Good room.

Under the sheet, the straining heat turns cold and then hot again. Fluids don't smell like anything until the vent decides they do. Tonight, the vent has chosen penny and candle.

My hands move like someone taught them. They did. Once. Long ago. Before the State cut the birthing floor into ghosts and rented its bones to this place.

I find the impossible truth with my fingers. Not flesh. Not head. Not bone. The thing crowning is not a person I have words for. It is cooler than skin and ridged like a bell mouth. It is small enough to hold and heavier than guilt.

"Don't," I tell the room. "Don't be clever." No one listens.

The contraction takes the decision away—the vent roars. The light over the table blares awake. The sheet goes scarlet and then white again, as if someone's editing the night for broadcast.

Something slides into my gloved palms.

It is a bell.

Brass, the color of old breath, wet the way new things are.

Tiny enough you'd use it to call a nurse. Heavy enough to keep a page from escaping. Its lip is etched with initials that aren't mine and mine: **M.H.** and **J.S.** The stem is wrapped in red thread wound so tight the metal squeaks when it tries to expand.

The bell rings once. Nothing moves. The sound happens anyway.

The monitor prints **APGAR: 10/10** like a comedian who's read the wrong script.

"Absolutely not," I tell the universe.

But the bell keeps going. Three small chimes and a pause. The census rhythm. The lullaby's last line.

I set it on the sterile drape because I don't know where else to put the child we made. The child we did not make. The child the building ordered because it could and because no one told it no when it learned how.

The sheet settles. The shape on the table breathes softer. I want to lift the linen and see. I don't.

"Congratulations," the intercom says in a man's voice that sounds like me if I knew how to be kinder. "Steward, you have a daughter."

The bell rings again like a laugh that isn't cruel. The monitor pings.

INFANT ID: M-13.

NAME: —.

MOTHER: Margaret Hale.

FATHER: Jack Steen.

ATTENDING MATRON: *Pending activation.*

A pale hand—mine—reaches for the bell and doesn't touch it. My hand stops. The air around the thing is warmer than my glove. The thread around the stem is no longer red. It's pinking toward white as if it's learned to be clean.

"Nurses," I say to no one and everyone. "I need nurses."

The hallway answers with wheels. The kind old bassinets used. Heavy, confident, awake after a long nap. They roll even though no one pushes them. They line up beside the table, three in a row, white sheets waiting with the arrogance of blank paper.

"Pick one," says the vent, in the Matron's voice, in my voice, in the place where both agree. "The first bed is for names. The second is for breath. The third is for counting."

"The fourth is for mercy," I say, because I want to remember I have that word. The vent doesn't argue. It has learned not to step on prayers said under your breath.

I choose the first crib because I know better than to trust breath. I know better than to trust numbers. Names keep people tethered. Names weigh less than a life and more than a confession.

I pick up the bell by its stem. It's lighter than it should be. Or my hand is stronger than it has any right to be tonight. The metal is warm against the glove. The sound it makes when the lip touches cotton is a sound your bones remember and your heart refuses to because if it remembered, you'd never stop.

The mobile above the crib turns—Moon, star, star, moon. Paper shadows print the word *STEEN* across the blanket and then a wind no one paid for erases it.

The intercom clicks. The pencil writes: *Complete.*

Steward confirmed. Matron successor—designation pending.

"Her name," I say. "What's her name?"

The ceiling chooses silence. Good ceiling.

I go back to the table. The sheet is neat again. Someone's tucked the corners the way the day shift likes. They tuck as if the battle is with a mess. Night tucks like the struggle is with forgetting. Both are correct and insufficient. My hands hover over the linen the way a blessing does when you're not sure of the recipient's consent.

"Ma'am?" I say to the room I keep accidentally calling a woman. "Do you need anything else?"

The vent exhales milk-scent and the smallest sound of a pencil reaching the end of a line and stopping there. The bell in the crib answers in a sleep-sound. Bells have sleep-sounds if you know what you're listening for.

I check the monitors. The second line—hers—reads 74, resolute. The top line—infant—ticks at **120** and then, like a new bird discovering wing, accelerates to **140** for one delighted second before settling back.

I reach for the chart. A new page has written itself while I blinked:

DISCHARGE PLAN:

Infant to remain on ward (M-13) *in situ.*

Mother *admitted* to the *ward, unknown.*

Steward to resume rounds.

Ledger to reflect *new account opened.*

The words <u>*new account opened*</u> are underlined in a hand that is not the administrator's. The underline is tidy and patient and refuses to end with a flourish because flourishes are how we apologize for meaning it.

Footsteps in the corridor. Soft soles, efficient, the music of people who know how to move without making the atmosphere angry. The light at the door lowers itself the way you dim a room before someone opens their eyes for the first time.

"Welcome back," the intercom says. The voice is a cheerfully dead-on imitation of my supervisor from four hospitals ago. I didn't like him then. I like him less as a ghost. "Please confirm attendance."

I pick up the recorder.

"Confirming attendance. Steen, Jack. Night nurse. Nursery floor."

I shouldn't feel proud. I do. Pride's a shape you make with your spine when you need to stay upright in a room that prefers otherwise.

The recorder clicks off by itself.

—

Back through the door—the not-elevator bites my shoulder in its desire to close. I pry it. The corridor makes a noise like someone clearing their throat out of habit. The callboard's red light dims to a pink that would be cute if I weren't on the wrong side of sane.

I push the nursery door open a last inch and look back. The cribs are still. The mobile stills. The bell sleeps. The sheet on the table lifts and falls in a rhythm that doesn't require my count anymore.

"Goodnight," I tell whatever we made. "Don't ring unless you mean it."

The vent listens. The vent decides to keep the lullaby for itself and hums only the last two notes so I'll know it can sing the rest.

I walk. The tile learns my pace. The hallway shortens politely

—the way a good host moves furniture for you without you having to ask. I get to the elevator and the button lights when I think about pushing it, which is great customer service from a building committed to poor outcomes.

Inside the car, I press **14** and get **12** first, as if the box wants to show me it remembers other ways down. The doors open onto my floor. The walls dare to be ugly again. The coffee in Security has overcooked itself to caramel and disappointment. Ike's voice in my head tells me to write it up, tell no one, and then tell him anyway.

I sit at my desk, and the chair remembers me like a dog that isn't allowed on the furniture.

03:11 —

I type a line into the incident log and watch it delete itself. In its place:

AUDIT: CENSUS_13 – SUBROUTINE "NURSERY" COMPLETE.

ACCOUNT: OPENED.

STEWARD: STEEN.

MATRON SUCCESSOR: PENDING.

The line winks into the system and hides. The printer coughs. I hear paperwork being born. I don't go get it. Not tonight. Not if I want to think I get choices.

The vent above my desk exhales. Candle and milk. The kind of smell that makes even the worst people remember they were once small and someone else had to decide if they got to keep.

I close my eyes. There it is—a cry. Not from the hall. Not from the duct. From somewhere behind my sternum. A small bright sound my chest throws like a stone into a lake, and then we both watch the circles widen.

"Absolutely not," I say. It ignores me, as we do good advice given too late.

I catch my reflection in the dark of the window over the parking lot. A nurse's cap sits on my head for precisely one impossible second, then remembers we don't wear those anymore and politely disappears. The hair underneath is mine and badly in need of a trim. The face underneath is mine and badly in need of plausible deniability.

The phone lights. A text from an unknown number because all numbers are unknown here.

Census complete. Nursery open. See you next year.

I text back **Who is this?** and **get Matron,** and then **read at 03:13 AM**.

"Sleep," I tell the building. It hums to humor me. It hums the part of the lullaby that lets fathers lie to themselves.

03:20 —

I lace my fingers together on the desk. They smell like metal under the latex. I take the gloves off, and the smell remains. I wash and it doesn't. The scent settles into the grooves of my fingerprints like a secret I promised not to repeat.

I leave the recorder where it can see me and speak like I'm not speaking to a wall.

"For the record: the maternity floor is open on Halloween, whether Administration admits it or not. A patient named Hale delivered an instrument that the hospital has decided to call a person. The instrument is a bell. The bell is a baby. Both of those sentences are true. No infant cries were heard — until I sat down."

I don't hit stop. The recorder hits stop like a friend who knows when I need the sentence to end.

The chapel bell rings not at all. The chapel has learned not to compete. Inside the duct, a small ding like someone pressing a service bell with a single, soft, proprietary finger kisses the air.

"Every number is a life," I say, because if I say it, I'm not pretending I wasn't there when a new one got added. "Every life is a record."

The vents agree by not disagreeing.

The clock on the wall sticks at 03:33 and then remembers to continue. I write the time in the log out of habit. There's ink under my nail. Red on first glance. Pinkish when I wipe it off. Thread burn, the kind you get when you pull too hard on something that doesn't want to let go yet.

I stand. The chair holds my shape a breath longer than it should. I look at the door to the hall and decide the hall can come to me if it needs something. I look at the ceiling and decide I don't mind being watched if the watcher has decent taste.

In the parking lot, the sodium lamps give up pretending to be morning and accept they are moons. A man in a coat walks his car to the curb like you walk a friend whose balance isn't sure. Somewhere, a nurse laughs a laugh she would never, ever waste on day shift.

I shut the light at my desk.

"Goodnight," I say to the floor above the floor above me. "Don't get clever."

A pause. Then, in the vent, a whisper that might be gratitude and might be an order: *Present.*

I answer the only way we're allowed to if we want to keep our jobs and our illusions.

"Present," I say. "Steen."

The building writes it down.

And somewhere, on a level that doesn't have to explain itself to blueprints, a very small bell tries out her voice.

ONLY JACK KNOWS: ORIGINS TO ANGELS

BEHIND the CONFESSIONS:

What started as a short audio series is now in book (and longer) audio! Consider these the 'behind the scenes' - stories that won't make it into any of the confession novels, but ones I still figured you'd enjoy.

Read, listen… and get ready for your next addiction. This one is only the beginning…

HAVE YOU READ THE HAUNTING SERIES YET?

THE HAUNTING OF GHOST LAKE
Chapter One
August 14, 1993

JAKE WILKINS

Jake wipes his clammy palms against his jeans as his foot eases just enough off the gas pedal. Maybe driving sixty down the dark, tree-lined dirt road isn't the smartest thing to do, regardless of David, his best friend, egging him on.

The last thing he wants to do is drive headfirst into one of these trees, thanks to a rut he can't see. His dad will kill him if he does, especially considering the old man helped buy this piece of junk.

"Slow down, asshole!" Mandy, David's girlfriend, barks out from the back. Jake glances at her through the mirror. She's got one hand touching the roof, the other giving him the finger.

Nice one. David sure knows how to pick the classy ones.

Despite being best friends, he doesn't get why David put up

166

with her bullshit. She's always bitching and complaining about any and everything Jake does. It's like his best friend is immune to her cattiness. Either that, or he's just ignoring it.

Ten to one, they don't last. Jake gives them two weeks, tops. A month, at the most.

Is he going a bit fast, hitting the bumps too hard, and making Mandy and Crystal, who are in the back seat, hit their heads on the roof? Of course, he is - but that's what makes it so much fun.

Besides, from the ass-grinning smile on David's face, he's enjoying this.

So why does he put up with Mandy? It doesn't hurt that she's so hot, with a pretty face and banging body. If anything, it's the blowjobs. It's what she's known for.

Jake glances in the rearview mirror at Mandy and her friend, Crystal. Mandy gives him a dirty look, then leans forward, setting her hand on David's shoulder, and whines, "Dave…"

David looks over at Jake with a *sorry man* type of look and suggests maybe slowing it down even more.

"Whatever." It doesn't matter anyway. Ghost Lake Sanatorium is just up ahead. The place has been neglected and abandoned for forty years or more. The sides of the building are black with age, and every window is broken, and most of them are boarded up. The front doors have slabs of wood nailed across them with huge DANGER, NO TRESPASSING signs on them.

Jake stops the car alongside the barbed wire fence that surrounds the building. The police are dumb if they think that's going to stop anyone from going inside and checking things out.

The stories about the sanatorium are too enticing not to see for yourself. He's been wanting to come forever, and yet…there's something about the place that has kept him away until now.

His leg bounces as he stares at the building up ahead. This place has a creep factor of *off-the-scale,* and from the way his heart beats against his chest, he's surprised everyone in the car can't hear how scared he feels.

One glance at David, and he's feeling it too. Jake wipes off all emotion from his face. The last thing he wants is for Mandy to notice.

She'd never let him live it down.

"Anyone see the monster?" Crystal leans forward, her hands gripping the front seats.

Last year, two middle schoolers snuck into the building and claimed they saw a shadow monster with glowing red eyes that chased them around. One of them had fallen through a hole in the front foyer and cut his leg as they ran out. His parents then went to the town council demanding more security be placed around the run-down building, ruining the experience for everyone else.

Coming here is a right of passage of sorts. What used to be a sanatorium for TB patients was then turned into a mental hospital for the criminally insane. What better place than out in the middle of nowhere, surrounded by mountains and a lake, in freaking northern Canada. Anyone who tried to escape died by natural causes - whether the wild animals or the cold, and those who didn't ended up on the chopping block of some insane doctor and nurse duo who sold their organs on the black market for profit.

It turns out money isn't the answer to everything because that duo was rumored to have been torn from limb to limb by a group of inmates in the late sixties.

"Well, are we doing this or what?" Mandy opens her door and gets out.

Jake can tell, despite her bravado, Mandy is scared shitless. So is Crystal, from the way she audibly swallows as she stares at the building, illuminated only by the bright full moon.

They all exit the car and gather in a group, a nervous energy pulsing between them.

Jake takes his shot, using this as the perfect situation to get close to Crystal. She's cute, not hot like Mandy, but there's more to her than just her smoking body. She's friendly, always ready with a smile for him, and with the cute little gap between her two front teeth, she's quite adorable. She's only ever given him the friends vibe, and that might be because he heard she hooked up with

Mike Langdon, a senior, about a month or so ago, but until she turns him down, he'll keep believing there's a makeup session happening between them tonight.

"Are you sure we won't get caught?" Crystal's voice shakes with uncertainty, which is funny since this was her suggestion.

"That's what makes it more exciting." Jake winks at her as he edges closer.

"Everyone ready?" Jake asks.

David reaches inside the car and and grabs a bag from the floor. In it is a bottle of vodka along with a jug of orange juice and some cups. "I am now."

"Now that's what I'm talking about," Mandy says as she places everything on the hood of Jake's car and mixes up the drinks. She passes everyone a cup, and they chug it back in a hurry, Jake especially, needing a little extra liquid courage if he's going to get close to Crystal.

"I thought you were bringing beer?" Jake says under his breath.

David shrugs. "This is all I could find. The vodka was at the back of the cupboard, so it won't get missed, and mom always buys extra orange juice for me."

Ever since they started hanging out in middle school, David has had an addiction to orange juice. On his own, he probably drinks a full jug every day. It's so bad that Jake's mom now keeps a jug of the juice in her fridge for when David comes over, which he does every day after school.

Once the buzz starts to set in, Jake takes out wire cutters from the car's trunk. "Always be prepared, as the old man says," he holds them up with a feeling of bravado.

Sniping a hole large enough for them all to climb through doesn't take much work. David goes first, then holds the fence for Mandy to crawl through after him.

Holding the fence open for Crystal, she's about halfway through before she backtracks.

"I almost forgot the whole reason why we're here," she says as she dashes back to the car. She returns, clutching a bag tight to her chest, and plants a little kiss on his cheek. "Thanks for waiting for me," she says.

"No problem," Jake mumbles as he watches her bend, giving him a perfect glance at her perfect ass.

Jake stays at the back of the pack as they walk toward the building, while David is up head, his steps way more eager than they should be.

David has been wanting to come here for ages, and it's always Jake who would find one excuse after another not to. So far, David hasn't caught on, at least, if he has, he hasn't said anything about it.

Seeing the place up close, Jake believes all the stories are true about this place. It has to be haunted; there's no other answer for the creepiness that lingers in the shadows as if those very tendrils are fingers just wanting to wrap themselves around the unsuspecting victims.

Victims like them.

If the girls weren't here, Jake would be hightailing it back to the car, David laughing at him be damned. This place gives off all the wrong vibes, and it's going to take a hell of a lot more alcohol to get him to walk through that door.

The closer they get, the more Jake wants to run. Fear finger walks its way up his spine, and he tries hard to suppress his shudder before anyone notices. Dread dances around him, its spikes catching on his jeans as he walks through the tall grass, and his stomach surges as he the imagery of skinless fingers poking up from the ground play with his head.

David races ahead and climbs up the rickety wood stairs, Mandy not too far behind him. She calls out to Jake and Crystal, telling them to hurry up. Crystal glances back toward Jake, her steps slowing as if waiting for him.

"You okay, slow poke?" Her eyes twinkle as she teases him.

All Jake can do is stare at her lips, remembering the touch of them on his cheek, and he swallows hard.

"Yeah, let's do this," he says with false bravado.

David grabs at the boards covering the door and, with the help of Mandy, pries a few away from the door.

"Jake man, come help," David says, grunting as he pulls harder.

It doesn't take much for the remaining boards to pop off. David tries the door handle, turning it one way, then the other, when they all hear a loud click, and the door nudges open as if on its own.

David jumps back with a 'huh' and then quickly laughs to cover up his surprise.

"Dude, the door was locked," David says to Jake.

"As if. Looks open to me."

"They must have forgotten to lock it when they boarded it up. Weird, huh?" Mandy says.

David nudges the door open wider just as an icy breeze blows over them, wrapping around their skin.

Both the girls yelp while David laughs. Jake joins in, but it's forced, and he prays to God that none of them notice.

The door slams shut just. They jump, and Crystal quickly grabs Jake's hand, squeezing hard.

David laughs again. "Maybe the place is haunted, and the spirits don't want us to come in," he teases as he nudges Mandy.

"Shut up, you asshole. That was probably just the wind closing the door, right?" Mandy glances back toward Crystal, then Jake.

He sees the challenge on Mandy's face, daring him to prove himself, unless he is too chicken, and if there's one thing he will not do, it's prove Mandy right.

David opens the door again, pushing it open hard enough that it hits the back of the wall, then slaps Jake on the back.

Is David scared too, but pretending to be brave for Mandy? If that's the case, Jake can do it too. Especially if it means Crystal doesn't let go of his hand.

"Come on, guys. You're not scared, are you?" David smirks, then steps through the open door.

For one split second, Jake almost doesn't do it. A shudder runs over his skin the second he steps across the threshold, and Jake's reminded of a comic he'd just read, where a group of kids walk into the gaping maw of some grotesque creature, and through the black hole of its mouth they're swallowed and morphed into hell.

Jake pulls out the flashlight he'd stuffed in his back pocket and turns it on, sweeping it back and forth along the walls and floors as they creep through the place.

The place is disgusting, with garbage everywhere, broken tables and chairs, and shards of glass crunching beneath their shoes. In one room, there's a single mattress on the floor, and he made the mistake of letting the light stay in one place, illuminating the dark stains. He doesn't want to think about what those stains were made from or how they were made.

"There's something wrong with this place," Crystal mutters to him. She released his hand a while ago, but she has yet to stray more than two feet away from him, which, to be honest, Jake is more than okay with.

Jake feels it, too. The air carries a thick layer of dread that coats his sweaty skin.

"Is anyone else here?" His voice squeaks as he asks the question.

"Seriously, dude?" David laughs as he turns and gives him one of those *what the fuck is wrong with you* looks.

"I feel it too," Crystal says, touching Jake's arm. "Like someone is watching us."

"Someone or something…" Mandy contorts her voice to sound like a witch, and Jake gives her the middle finger.

They can laugh all they want, but the thick layer of goosebumps over his skin tells a different story.

Someone or something is here with them. Watching him.

Not just him but all of them.

A steady scratch-like nails on a chalkboard combined with the sound of a dozen rats scurrying about, Jake turns in circles, trying to determine where the sound is coming from. If it's rats, they're definitely in the walls, and yet, the sounds are both above his head and right beneath his feet.

Crystal gasps and jumps. "Something just touched my ankle."

David laughs, but he doesn't sound as sure as before. "Come on, don't be stupid. You're just letting the place get to you. Those sounds are just rats. The cold draft is from an opening somewhere. That's it. The rest are just stories someone made up to keep kids away."

Jake copies his laugh. "Yeah, probably."

"Come on. I hear there are tunnels beneath us. Now that would be the perfect place for our thing tonight. After all, this was your idea, Crystal, right?"

Crystal hugs the bag she'd brought close to her chest and steps away from Jake.

"Let's do this."

THE ECHOES OF SIN - A JACK ORIGINAL

THE ECHOES OF SIN

This one is a little different but I wanted to let you know about this book. If you like anything supernatural - think angels and demons, nephalim and a spiritual war - then you might enjoy this book. It was the first one I've ever written and my VIP Addicts group convinced me to publish it so everyone could read it.

I hope you enjoy it!

CONFESSION BOOK - THE ORIGINALS

The Asylum Confessions

The one that started it all! These are a few of my favorite confessions - if you haven't already read them, I hope you enjoy the journey!

JOIN ME

Don't forget - there will be more books.

But while you wait, why not join me over on my VIP ADDICTS group?

What happens over there? A lot. Like…you read these confessions before anyone else. Like…you get to name characters. Like…you get free books.

It's also a better way to stay in touch rather than a mailing list that you may or may not see in your inbox.

https://www.patreon.com/jacksteen

Click to check it out…no pressure, but if you do sign up, be sure to say hello in one of the posts, and I'll raise a toast to you at the pub.